KENYON, MICHAEL.
THE SHOOTING OF DAN
MCGREW /
1975, C
37565009122812   CENT

W9-CRE-248

CENTRAL

The Shooting
of Dan McGrew

7322

M

The Shooting
of Dan McGrew

Michael Kenyon

P. 7e

David McKay Company, Inc.
Ives Washburn, Inc.
New York

The Shooting of Dan McGrew

COPYRIGHT © 1972 BY MICHAEL KENYON

All rights reserved, including the right to reproduce
this book, or parts thereof, in any form, except for
the inclusion of brief quotations in a review.

First American Edition, 1975

LIBRARY OF CONGRESS CATALOG CARD NUMBER: 75-7905
ISBN 0-679-50553-9
MANUFACTURED IN THE UNITED STATES OF AMERICA

CHAPTER I

The crazed prospector, ice on his beard, lurched through the swing doors into the saloon's glare. The laughing and cursing, the jangling of the mechanical piano, faded to silence. All eyes turned on the stranger. With a dying effort he lifted high his leather poke, turned it so that gold nuggets poured like gravel to the floor, and falling to his knees, croaked, 'I guess I'll make it a spread misère.' Then gunfire blasted the lights, all hell broke loose, and such was the din that Detective-Superintendent O'Malley awoke with a pain in his ears.

He climbed out of his bachelor bed, scratched, and padded into the kitchen for cornflakes. It was morning anyway, and ahead lay a destroying class of a day on the sweepstake fraud. In the street below, the Dublin dustmen were demonstrating to each other with emptied dustbins, dustbin lids and a baked bean tin how Larry Mulcahy had scored his third and finest at Croke Park. Superintendent O'Malley carried his cornflakes into the sitting-room and plucked from the bookshelf a 1907 edition, bequeathed by his mother, of *Songs of a Sourdough*.

Robert Service, yerrah, there was a fella knew how to string the words together. The Canadian Kipling, someone had called him. Seated in an armchair, dripping milk through the open neck of his pyjamas, O'Malley munched and read. It hadn't, he discovered, been the miner fresh from the creeks who'd guessed he'd make it a spread misère, it had been Dangerous Dan McGrew himself, back of the bar in a solo game.

McGrew, reflected O'Malley. Ah. That was why he had dreamed McGrew. Dan McGrew, hadn't that been the name of one of the missing mining engineers down in Carrigann? Who was the other—Hayling, Harlow? Canadians, both.

Well, they weren't his pigeon, not unless he was asked, and he hoped to God he'd not be because the older he grew the less stomach he had for the violent stuff, and there was a sticky smell of violence in Carrigann. The sweep fiddle, that was more his territory.

A soggy milky cornflake dripped into the grey hair of the Superintendent's chest as he read on about blazing guns, betrayal and violence in the Malamute saloon.

'McGrew, Harvey, how do I know,' said Skipper Ogden, 'if I let you go, Henry, you won't be number three?'

'You're the boss,' Henry Butt said, uneasy in the feeling that the words were not his but someone's in the late-late movie through which last night, sated with crab quenelles, he had yawned, shrunk, and finally slept. He fingered his scalp through its clipped curly red hair. 'I mean, I don't mind. There must be a rational explanation. I'll go if you like. Whatever you think.'

'Whatever *you* think.' Skipper Ogden, President, Ogden Enterprises (Akron, Ohio) Inc., pointed. 'You're the boss, Henry. On this ship, we're structured for individual decision-taking. Each sailor is captain of his own soul. The admiral we all must answer to, the man on the bridge, is Almighty God. Isn't that right, Conrad?'

'Yes,' yessed Conrad.

Yes, well, I really don't mind, I'd be happy to go,

Henry considered. By the time he arrived in Carrigann, McGrew and Harvey probably would have shown up. Henry located through his hair the whatever that itched.

'We've lost,' Ogden was saying, 'two good men in two weeks in that benighted goddam Ireland. Only temporarily lost, maybe, God grant it's only temporarily. But I'm not figuring on losing you too, Henry. If you want to know—' and Ogden paused while the conference furrowed its brows, wanting to know—'I'm in two minds. I'm considering closing the whole Carrigann shebang.'

Shebang, shebeen, mused Henry. A jar of porter and a terrible beauty is born.

Henry Butt's experience of Europe was limited to a misbegotten year of peacetime foot-soldiering in Wiesbaden plus three expensive weeks' leave in France, but he was game. Though Ireland would not have been his first choice, there would be the chance of excursions to the fleshpots of Paris. Literally, fleshpots : swimming *sauté de veau de campagne, rognons flambés au Métro Denfert-Rochereau, pommes frites truffés.* He could see the chequered tablecloths, smell the Gauloises, the garlicky ambience ('Garçon, another ladle of that splendid garlicky ambience!') Under his tongue gathered the juices. Far away those fleshpots from fieldwork in Mexico and Arizona, benchwork in the Toronto laboratory; but now, seemingly, accessible.

'Who needs that cruddy Carrigann anyway? What's going on?' Ogden Enterprises wanted to know.

The something on the scalp was, Henry discovered, the minusculest scab, a paltry nothing, a fribble. Where he had stabbed himself, he supposed, with the comb, after the morning's hairwash.

'First McGrew, now Harvey!' Skipper Ogden slapped the conference table. Vice-presidents, tall executives, consultants, accountants, and Henry Butt, jumped. 'McGrew, okay, I never met McGrew. Come to that I never met Harvey. A guy's greatest regret on reaching my position is that he can't meet the whole crew. The fleet is scattered, there are too many sailors. It's a deprivation.' The anointed boss of Ogden Enterprises did not, in Henry's view, look deprived. The latest press photograph, four days old, had shown Ogden striding through forest with cradled sixteen-bore, under the other arm some kind of deceased animal, and behind him a retinue of gillies with staves and hampers. 'Harvey has sailed with Ogden's a dozen years. Hasn't he? A loyal, devoted shipmate. What's more he has a wife, a lovely, lovely lady.'

'McGrew,' Conrad said.

'What?' said Ogden.

'McGrew has the wife, Skipper. Marylene.'

'See what I mean? It's a goddam shambles.'

'Can't,' said a consultant accountant, 'the Irish police turn up anything?'

Ogden capsized the Irish police with a sailor's oath. The accountant consulted his finger-ends, a manicurist passing judgement. 'Tell you what I think,' Ogden snarled. 'Nancy boys. Fags!'

'Ireland's rife with it,' a vice-president agreed. 'It was bound to get to the police. Inverts, all of them.'

'I'm talking about Harvey and McGrew,' Ogden said. He pointed: a bowsprit aimed at Henry's skull. 'You, Henry, you're not even married. Why?'

Henry withdrew a startled fist out of the washed red scalp. 'I'm not saying it hasn't come up,' he said. 'Anyway, what about the gun?'

'We'll find you a gun,' Ogden said. 'You'll be wanting a recoil-less rifle to defend your honour against those Mick cops.'

While Skipper Ogden swayed with laughter, and the conferees laughed on cue, flapping their elbows and turning to each other windy, teeth-clacking mouths, Henry groped in a pocket and brought out his snuff tin. He wondered whether the president of Ogden Enterprises might be odder than he seemed on this initial acquaintance, or less odd but more eerie.

Unlike Henry's curly cropped hair, Skipper Ogden's hung black and lank over his ears, compensation for a fashion which had been unavailable in his youth. Under the business suit he wore an unsuitable cerise silk sweater with turtle-neck. Financial potentate, and more recently gubernatorial prospect for the Buckeye State of Ohio, the closest Skipper Ogden had ever come to the sea was 50,000 feet up in cushioned jets transporting him to Buenos Aires, Tokyo, Madrid and the score of depots where lay his overseas interests. In North America, the complexity of interests was known only to himself and the US Treasury Department (Internal Revenue Service), which knew less than it would have liked, and knew it knew less, but was deterred from learning more by knowledge of the cost, time and tears that would have been entailed in learning more. Half a dozen times annually, self-made Skipper Ogden would sweep across the border to his Toronto office, and now that Henry, a fieldworker normally far-flung from the Toronto base, was encountering this remote employer for the first time, he was unable to fathom whether the man had as much chance for the governorship of Ohio as a fruit bat, or whether he was as good as in. According to the political pages Ogden was running on a peace-and-disarmament ticket which to Henry was at odds with the man's bursts of pugnacity, and not entirely in tune with the political climate. Except that some political pages thought the politicial climate was changing so fast that Ogden would not only surf in to the Ohio governorship but possibly to the White House in the next presidential election but one.

Not that American politics were any concern of Henry's. All he felt confident about was that Ogden, promising politician or not, was no geologist. Ogden would not have known an igneous pegmatite from Plasticine.

'Zinc, forty-two point eight nine per cent; lead, five point forty per cent.' Ogden quoted aloud from a file labelled, Ivernia Exploration Co. 'Henry?'

'Aaaaaaaaaaaghssssssh!' sneezed Henry as the snuff smote the membrane.

'Put that goddam stuff away, you junkie, and say whether five point forty is worth going ahead with.'

'Well worth it, I'd say,' said Henry.

'It's over a month old, February twenty-third, and the last word from McGrew before he went pansying off.' Ogden spun the file over the table top for salvaging by anyone who was keen. 'Fine, so it put another dollar on the shares, we're all rich. But I've got a reputation—tune in at eleven tomorrow, CBS—and I quit Carrigann, wind it up, sell, burn it down, whatever it takes, before I lose another rock-head. How about it, Henry? Suppose you go to Carrigann? Do you go missing?'

Rock-head was the Skipper's endearment for geologist;

Carrigann the field in County Cork where rock-heads from Ivernia Exploration, an Ogden Enterprises subsidiary, were prospecting then going missing. Ivernia Exploration held a dozen prospecting licences in scattered Irish fields. Some, well beyond the exploratory stage, were locating in greater or lesser quantities, lead; others copper and zinc; one in County Limerick had caught a whiff of silver. Only at Carrigann had prospectors vanished, a drilling rig been smashed, the gardai stepped in, and Garda Inspector Mulligan tripped immediately over a gun.

Henry sought the fribble in his scalp, and a vice-president began a monologue on the gun, which Mulligan had not discovered, the vice-president revealed, a gardener had discovered, then handed over, larded from handle to spout with his green-fingered fingerprints. And where had he found said gun (Exhibit One)? In the herbaceous border fifty feet below Danny McGrew's room at the Kilkelly Castle Hotel, twelve miles from Carrigann. The same castellated, over-upholstered hotel from which had now vanished, before he had had time even to look at the Carrigann site, McGrew's successor, Harvey, PhD (Univ. of Col.). Did that, the gun, and the busted drill, and the twin disappearances look like mere faggotry? To the Irish cops it looked like foul play, exclaimed the light-shedding vice-president, starting to tremble. His name was Butane and he was the only conferee to have pursued the matter through its day-by-day newspaper paragraphs.

'For God's sake, Butane, shut up,' Ogden said.

The Toronto boardroom was hot and sweaty. A consultant smoked a cigar with an ebony mouthpiece like an oboe. Henry, gently as a mother, rocked the fribble.

Puberty, some twenty-five years ago, had come to him late, and like most late developers he had continued growing, arms and legs especially, long after most of his contemporaries had stopped. In recent years excessive intake of calories had added bulk to height. An insignificant freckled nose supported gold-rimmed glasses with deeply concave lenses, thin at the centre, thickening towards the periphery, which made his eyes look like two lentils.

Tipping back his protesting chair and gazing sideways, Henry could see through the picture-window the lake and a portion of Island Park. He heard a bark. Ogden was lunging the bowsprit.

'Henry?'

'Aye-aye, sir.'

'You don't look to me like the bearded Klondike bear-type prospector.'

'No?'

'So make up your mind. I can give you the survey at Sacramento, or you can flog on in the Sierra Mojada, God help you. But I'll tell you my motto, the motto of Ohio, and hand in hand together, Henry, me and you Canadians can maybe go places. "With God All Things Are Possible." Okay? So if you must go to goddam Ireland and get yourself perverted and shot and rained on—that's right, Henry, in Ireland it rains—don't come crying to Skipper Ogden.'

'When would I go?'

Ogden shrugged. 'We're behind schedule.'

Henry infinitesimally dilated a nostril. He could almost smell the spicy sidetrips to the *fricasée de bonne bouche en aspic*. Thyme, he mused, was of the essence.

CHAPTER II

Half-past six on a rainy April evening in the Palm Room of the Kilkelly Castle Hotel. Kate Kennedy, spinster, open handbag on her lap beneath the table, pretended to search for cosmetics, an important key, letters from dear friends. Secretly she counted her money.

Sixty pounds in tens, the fiver, a fifty-pence piece which would be sucked up in tonic waters over the next half hour, and a shoal of nonsense. Plus the ten tens under the wall-to-wall carpeting of her room made a hundred and sixty-five. A hundred and sixty-five divided by room, meals and service at sixteen pounds per day. That made (Kate had done the sum before, many times) ten more days and the fare home. Fourteen days if she cancelled the evening meal and bought a tin of biscuits and a packet of tea.

Kate shivered. She wondered if she might be getting a temperature. She knew, no question of wondering, she had lost her senses. Two days gone, another ten to go (fourteen with biscuits), misery, loneliness, humiliation, a probable temperature, a life's savings sinking at the rate of sixteen pounds per day into the bottomless maw of the Kilkelly Castle Hotel, and not a husband in view. She clipped shut the bag and pretended to enter social engagements in her diary. Secretly she surveyed the strays in the Palm Room.

A displaced touring couple, boy and girl, who had dropped in out of curiosity and would be off like smoke once they saw their bill for gin and olives. The golfing foursome from Laredo or wherever, sprawled round a table and chewing in soft voices over the day's birdies. The swart male twosome who were too young and never spoke to anyone anyway, hardly even to each other. The tottering etiolated English couple who had asked her the previous evening if she would stand by for bridge if they could find a fourth, and at 8.45 p.m. had retired sensibly to bed. Mulligan, the bald policeman, at the bar with orangeade, talking to the hotel's owner, Ramsey Gore. And that was all.

The full April complement, assembled. If there were others they were out in the rain, or in their rooms, eschewing the cocktail hour. The Belfast party with fishing rods and tins of worms, for instance, and the cheerful man from the Tourist Board who had spoiled it by giving her that odious glad-eye, had they all gone?

The Palm Room had space for another hundred guests. Three similar lounges with different sobriquets were totally deserted, their radiators cold. Much of her first day at the Kilkelly Castle, Kate had spent sidling from one public room to another, asking herself where the action was. Now, as she surveyed, she was resigned to its absence. April was too soon, she should have waited till midsummer. But come midsummer the tariff would rocket. In midsummer she could have afforded perhaps three days, without food. Three days with gait progressively enfeebled as malnutrition took hold, eyeballs withdrawing into bony sockets. These were terrible handicaps for landing a husband.

Kate's only serious handicap to landing a husband was, in fact, her defeatism, as any psychologist, or in-

deed any sober heterosexual male could have told her.
Her character was sound, her disposition generous, her
health good, and her wits, apart from the lapse of this
mad excursion to Kilkelly, anchored more or less in
reality. Physiologically she was not built after the grand
design of Miss Ireland, but for anyone with an eye for
the smaller-boned woman, black-haired and wide-eyed,
there was no more fetching catch in all Munster. Her
seven sisters and brothers were married, however, and
here was the crunch. Already Kate was eighteen times
an aunt, and as she advanced into her mid-thirties she
became more and more ready to write off her unmarried
state as God's will. Any generalizer might have pointed
out that this defeatism was a peculiarly Irish trait, probably incurable. Even her presence at Kilkelly signified,
ironically, defeatism; indeed this was the very bedrock
of pessimism, as not for one moment did Kate believe
that suitors were about to converge on her. Here was
Kate at her extremity, indulging herself with a final desperate gesture prior to settling down to fifty years of
spinsterdom. Round the edge of the lifted tonic bubbles
she watched the absence of action.

The displaced touring couple were rising, she gathering about her shoulders a furry poncho, he dealing
banknotes to the barman, Brian. Now they were departing with shaken expressions, out to their Triumph Spit-
fire and sullen memories of life's, and the Kilkelly Castle
Hotel's, confidence trick. Brian, nineteen years old and
beautiful in a malachite-green jacket with KCH em-
broidered in 72pt Century Bold Italic over the left
breast, returned behind his bar to induce chiming noises
out of the till. Manager Ramsey Gore (KCH, Kate

assumed, carved upon his brass heart), was reaching his
arms in front of him, measuring what seemed to be the
dimensions of a tuna for an impassive Mulligan.

Kate's question was: should she stick it out, or cut
her losses and leave in the morning.

To leave in the morning would be to admit defeat,
though not annihilating defeat. But to thrash on and
return home in penury, still defeated, would leave pride
and nervous system scarred until the end of her days.

Yet to stay would be the act of a crazy woman. With
the hundred and sixty-five pounds saved by retreat she
could live at home in Ennis for three or four months,
by the end of which period she might be earning money
in a shop or hotel. And her father's will might have
been proved. Not that that would be anything to jig
about once her brothers and sisters had swept up their
share.

But in Ennis were no husbands. Not, that was to say,
unmarried husbands. Some young ones were coming on
but they were not of her generation. Kate had lived
thirty-four years in Ennis, she had never lived anywhere
else, and she knew.

She sipped her tonic water, pretending it to be spiked
with vodka. Secretly she not only detested vodka but was
not much enjoying the tonic water. Glances were turned
her way but no one rose to approach her and offer
company.

Suddenly she was alert. The swart twosome had
swapped monosyllables. From her table by the window
Kate could not hear the monosyllables, but one of the
twosome had leaned towards the other and opened his
mouth. Now they were leaning back again, mouths

shut, except intermittently to allow in whatever the pink medicine in their glasses was. Their suits shimmered expensively but their faces were those of costing clerks from the more southerly reaches of the Common Market, and they were too young. Probably they didn't even speak English. They sat at a table by the far wall under a giant painting of red circles. Thousand upon thousand of red circles.

Not even to Father Fahy would Kate have confessed that she had written to the Kilkelly Castle Hotel on the day following her father's funeral. Before he was cold in his grave. It had been a toss-up between the sham turrets and pinnacles of Kilkelly, of which she had seen photographs in Come to Ireland advertisements, and the more obvious coliseums of Cork and Dublin. Partly she had thought she would prefer country after the pace of Abbey Street, Ennis, where her widowed optician father had peered into eyes and groped among his cases of lenses for too many years after the point where he himself could see no more than a blur. More considerably, she had reasoned that at the plush watering-holes of St Stephen's Green, eligible guests might be preoccupied with business deals or sight-seeing. In the country, guests would be looking about them, horse-riding perhaps by day, in the evening flexing their social muscles. Males at Kilkelly would be inclined to camaraderie, gallantry, the striking up of friendships which might even prove (praise God) permanent. The country males, moreover, would be as rich as the city males, if not richer.

Not that Kate was mercenary. But if a girl hoped to marry she might as well try to marry into comfort. During a life of housekeeping she had grown acquainted with dreams of a housekeeper of her own, and if possible a cook, and a six-bedroomed house to which her husband would return each evening saying, 'Shall we go to a First Night tonight, darling, or would you prefer bezique? After, of course, kissing good night our many and adorable children.'

Kate watched, covertly, the Texans, or Californians, or South Nebraskans. She had an uneasy impression that when she was not watching them they watched her, covertly. They were the best bet, indeed the only bet (she was definitely not about to marry a policeman, or the pompous Ramsey Gore, now miming the dimensions of a brill), but she could not deny that they were a bet only for lack of competition. Apart from the paunchy one, who looked fiftyish and was, she believed, a doctor, they must have all been beyond a well-married sixty. The fiftyish one glanced her way, catching her eye. Kate looked hastily down, lifted her glass, sipped.

A week after receiving postal confirmation of her room, she had read in her Ennis newspaper of police activity at the hotel. A gun had been found, a Canadian mining engineer had vanished. Only two weeks ago the newspaper had reported the disappearance from Kilkelly of a second mining engineer. Kate's heart had lifted. Perhaps distinguished, unmarried editors would be arriving at the hotel, and more mining engineers.

Of course the reality was different. Alone, she could not even include herself in debates on the vanished mining engineers, if they were being debated. She had tried with Brian but all he would say was, "Tis a mystery all right.' The random dropping-in of the garda man was, so far as Kate could see, the only indication that anything mysterious had happened, and he had made no attempt to interrogate her.

Brian was unloading fresh drinks for the American foursome. When he looked in Kate's direction she nodded and touched her glass. Turning her head she could see through the window, through the rain, beyond the drive, acres of undulating parkland, green as Brian's jacket. There were fir trees, elms and oaks, a bit of lake, and a distant sodden pennant marking the seventh green. No golfers though, tanned aristocrats who later in the evening would carry her off. No limousines purring up the drive with consignments of potential husband-fodder. Kate softly burped, and giggled.

The situation had its wild side. For the first time in two days Kate felt she had a joke to share. Desperate, virgin Kate (she did not count the tussle, at nineteen, with the Gallagher boy in his mother's parlour, or the extraordinarily stimulating though limited encounters with Peter Lynch, a decade later), gambling her all—self-esteem, confidence, bank balance—on this ludicrous jaunt to Kilkelly. Holed up in the plush like a dowager. In a vacuum, in the company of vacuous nothings in trousers. Not even in their company, thanks be to God! It was not, Kate was starting to realize, that she was all that desperate to be married.

She would ask for her bill in the morning. Her mind was made up.

The stupidity! Sitting waiting like a cow at an auction, and all the bidders blind and paralysed.

Brian set down a fresh tonic water and hovered, awaiting the chat which Kate normally embarked on. But she offered the merest inclination of her head.

Puzzled, Brian retired. Birds, never knew where you stood with them.

Kate sipped. Over the tonic bubbles she watched walking into the Palm Room a newcomer, a very large man with curly red wet hair which must have lately surfaced from a scalding bath. The man hesitated, blinking and smiling as though uncertain whether or not he should utter a public greeting. He sat abruptly at the table nearest him, blinking through gold-rimmed pebble-lensed glasses.

I'll collect my bill tonight, Kate decided.

CHAPTER III

McGrew's handwriting was cramped and ovular, like a tray of eggs.

Dear Marylene,

I am writing this in a deserted lounge in my hotel which as you can see is the Kilkelly Castle Hotel, though it is more a Hotel than a Castle. If it was ever a Castle someone has made alterations. Still it is a bit of OULD OIRELAND. In the Lobby they have these kind of clubs or Shilalies, or maybe Shilaylees, you can buy them, and likewise Leprachaun Dolls, I'll bring you back one. They get Life and Newsweek (but not Mac-leans) so we're not completely 'in the bogs' but this Hotel is the only one for twenty miles round, I guess till you get to Cork, and it's pretty ritzy in a desolate way. Don't worry, we're not paying. So everything is okay though the weather is lousy so let me tell you what has hap-

pened since I left T. The flight was the usual . . .

Half-way through the first page, Henry Butt flipped over to see how much more. Two, no three sheets. Towards the end, happily, the eggs became bigger. The narrative seemed impersonal enough, but Henry felt a distaste for this peeping into another's private life. An Ogden aide had passed him photo-copies of the two letters from McGrew to his wife ('These'll fill you in, Henry'), and but for having packed them in a suitcase which he had handed in at Toronto Airport, he would have been shut of them by now.

Henry glanced across the Palm Room at the woman sitting alone by the window, studying a diary. Who was she waiting for?

. . . car to the Kilkelly Castle Hotel . . . driving on the left like there is nothing to it, it is a question of instant adjustment . . . Limerick, over the Ballyhoura Hills, then Kilkelly . . . pretty enough but dead, I hope I last out . . . Mr Gore . . . they get us Canucks over for golf in the summer, and of course Americans . . .

Suddenly, a page of items forgotten, left behind in the old homestead : *the wool jersey with the ribbing, the stop-watch, the waterproof boots maybe in the closet in the rumpus room . . . and Marylene, would you send them on?* Henry skimmed the forgotten items.

He risked a second sip from his glass of red wine. It was as unsatisfactory as the first, gritty with a bouquet of paperhanger's adhesive. The wine wasn't even red : more brown. Indeed, if held up to the light (Henry held it up to the light) it reflected a chromatic scale of browns from Vandyke at the surface, with the merest hint of henna, shading through khaki, chocolate and sepia, and darkening to sloe at the bottom, where the grit lay. Wherever it had travelled from it had travelled too far. On the other hand, maybe it had not travelled far enough. The best solution, Henry reflected, would have been for it to keep on travelling, on and on, a stateless wine turned away at each port of entry, a Wandering Jew of the vineyards, a vagabond of the vendange, without ancestry or papers, properly rejected, a sempiternal passenger in quest of haven, ever in transit, leaving in its wake its paperhanger's aroma and Customs officers muttering over the insolence, and finally, finally—excited by this forecast for his glass of wine, Henry started drumming his fingers on the table—going into orbit round its vintner's skull.

Still, he did not want to make a fuss his first evening. The slight brunette in tweeds was gazing through the window, a little aimlessly, in Henry's opinion. Where was the husband? Caught in the rain, no doubt, his car trapped by floodwaters, a damp distributor. It was not right she should sit alone, she must feel slightly uncomfortable, mustn't she? Henry liked the black, severely brushed hair, the exiguous nose. Her mouth was wide, a little too wide to be in proportion, and he liked that too. The hands he liked. The tweed jacket and skirt were pearl-grey (which he liked), but he could not tell the colour of her eyes. Should he offer her a glass of wine?

The eyes (ultramarine? mahogany?) met his. They looked immediately elsewhere, as did Henry's.

Dear Marylene,

I am wondering if you got my first letter of about three weeks ago. There are a few things I forgot to bring. I have bought new boots because it is pretty damn muddy on the Site but if you could find . . .

Henry skimmed the recapitulation. He realized he had not yet finished the first letter, returned to it, discovered nothing of moment, and came back to the second.

The woman was drinking something colourless. A tippler? A divorcée perhaps? Anyway, a lovely, lovely girl, Henry thought. Was it the eyes? The colouring?

. . . so let me tell you about Carrigann. It is a dozen miles from the Hotel, there is the village, such as it is, and our hundred acres pretty well surround it. Most of the land is farmed by a guy called Boland and we have problems with his livestock. There are three Pubs, a couple of Groceries, a Post Office where you can buy milk and cream and this Guinness drink, and that is about it. The Church, of course, and a gas pump, and I must tell you some time about the gas pump. Most of the cottages are white but some and the shops are painted in these colours I have never seen before. The Priest has a good-looking place and there are some big houses out a bit, but Carrigann itself is as one-horse as you can get. Like there is no special reason it should be there except it always has been.

Well, that is the point. As you know we have been getting such good results that Carrigann will soon be 'on the map', I am sure of that. It is already two-horse since Ivernia moved in, and you never can know but if we go on 'hitting it' like the hole we sank Wednesday it may soon look like a cavalry charge. Ivernia is front page news here! All the locals are buying if they have two cents to rub together (and though you would not think it, my guess is some of them have plenty). I am not saying it is good old Dawson City in '98 but you remember when Jim Butler made the first assay for us and got 38 zinc and 5 lead, then the Skipper pulled him out for that mad Sacramento survey—half the time that nut Ogden doesn't know what he is doing, I have always said so—then he sent me, well, Hole 8 has given us the best yet—49 per cent lead and zinc combined. In fact we drilled 345 ft and the best 50 ft averaged 52.8! So what I am saying is my advice is sell your Pellco Hold-inbs AND the Edmonton, neither is doing a thing, and buy Ivernia now while they are peanuts. You know I am Old Mister Caution about the Market but if you want to know what I am doing I cabled Dick yesterday to say trade all my DKD-Sintex, all the Int. Oil and Gas, and half the Guadalajara (I cling to Hudson's Bay for sentiment's sake!) and buy Ivernia. Fact is, but you must keep this absolutely dark, there may be some-thing else here. Keep this 'under your hat'. I am not saying more because it would not be fair to you to have the responsibility and anyway I am not certain, but I think I am on to something pretty damn weird. I will be working 'flat out' for the next few days. Even if my guess is 'off the beam' . . .

Henry frowned. Silver? In Limerick there were traces of silver, for what it was worth. Gold in Wicklow, but not a chance of it in Cork, not unless the geological memoirs had been written by a travel agent. Copper? Nickel? Impossible.

. . . there is enough lead and zinc mineralization under this Ould Sod to warrant you buying now. Do not put it off, because the price will shoot. The thing is this forsaken Carrigann is slap on the River Awbeg, which

*is a tributary of the Blackwater and would get the ore
either to Mallow or Fermoy, and from there to Cork
would be easy. Apart from lack of 'high life' for the
poor prospector—and frankly I am not going to have
much time for that—Carrigann could not be better
situated.*

*Monday night I drove to Cork with some Americans
here and we had a steak at a place called the Oyster
and took in a movie, Lee Marvin, which was okay, but
that has been pretty well it to date social-wise. I don't
see myself getting home for at least the next couple of
months, maybe early May, but if Ivernia shares do
what they should do you could fly to Shannon . . .*

Endearments through which Henry skimmed, and the
signature, *Dan.* Henry summoned a smile for the barman.

'Don't think I'm complaining but I'd like your honest
opinion.' Henry slid the wine towards Brian. 'Would you
taste that?'

'Thanks all the same, sir, I don't.'

'No, only taste, you don't have to drink. It's information I'm after.'

'Try Reception, sir. They've a stack of leaflets.'

'Please, I want you to tell me what you think. Try it.'

'Well, thank you very much, sir, I'll have a bottle of
stout.'

'What I mean is, is all your wine like this?'

'Is it not very nice?'

'That's right. Where did you get it?'

''Twas on the shelf.'

'Opened?'

'Not at all. The cork was in it.'

'How long,' Henry inquired slowly, carefully, 'has it stood half empty, or full, which is to say half full, or thereabouts, on the shelf?'

'Christmas?'

'Christmas!'

'We don't have much call for wine, y' see. We're not what you might call a wine-drinking community.'

'Would you have just one other wine apart from this? Anything? Unopened?'

'I have, I'm sure.'

'A wine list?'

'I'll take a look.' Brian picked up Henry's abandoned glass and sniffed it. 'You say this one isn't so grand?'

'I'm afraid not.'

'What's' (sniff) 'its trouble?'

'Metal fatigue.' Henry was aware of evaporating interest.

'It has a queer oul' smell.' Brian's interest mounted. 'No question about that. You don't want to be drinking stuff like this.'

'Right.'

'I'll give it to the chef.'

'He'll get the palsy.'

'He's already got it. Would you like to see the menu?'

'No, thank you.'

'Just the wine list?'

'I suppose so.'

'I'll tell you what.' Brian sniffed the wine with enthusiasm. 'I'll not charge you for this one.'

He weaved away between tables, infrequent guests and empty armchairs, holding the glass of wine like an alchemist with an ingredient for the elixir of life. Henry put McGrew's letters into an inside pocket.

When Brian returned it was not with a wine list but with a wine glass, corkscrew and a bottle of claret.

The English couple sat stiff as sculptures, sizing up Henry as a potential bridge-player and suffering doubts as they watched him pour his second glass from the wine bottle.

Ramsey Gore had departed, leaving Inspector Mulligan alone at the bar sipping his sixth orangeade, chewing upon his limited facts, and wishing Dublin would send one of their sharp brains.

The golfing foursome debated the pros and cons of an excursion to the links at Portmarnock.

Speechless, the swart Common Market clerks sat.

Kate sat computing with pencil and paper her bill to date.

'Pardon me.'

Kate looked up in alarm. The shiny, red-haired newcomer loomed over her.

'I mean until your husband arrives, just a passing thought, if you'd care to,' Henry said, registering too late the naked, unringed fingers, 'I have this, ah, well, I'm no expert, you understand, but you seemed to be alone, just temporarily, it's a pretty useful wine.'

CHAPTER IV

'Château Margaux,' Henry said. 'That's a vineyard in Bordeaux, a famous one, and the red Bordeaux wines are clarets, so this is a claret. Margaux is in the Médoc.'

'You just said it was in Bordeaux.'

'Yes, good, it is, the Médoc is a region of Bordeaux, and Margaux, where this comes from, is a commune. In the Médoc.'

'It's a rare old tangle. You don't imagine I'll remember all that.'

'I'll draw a map.'

They sat at Kate's table with the wine and an additional wine glass supplied by a discreetly quizzical Brian. Kate suspended judgement. At least the man was clean, too clean if anything, his pink skin glistening, his soap-smell overwhelming what he kept referring to as the wine's nose. Henry, wine-tasting, drawing France's Atlantic seaboard on a blank patch of McGrew letter, had decided that when the Margaux was finished, which would be soon, he could call for a Pomerol, or maybe St Emilion, something lighter, so that she might see the difference. Not only was this woman extraordinarily intelligent, sympathetic, discriminating, modest, warm, receptive, mature and charming, she was also, or had been until he had crossed the floor, alone. There was no reason why they should not become friends. And later, after the ice-breaking, dare he ask her to share his table at dinner? She might even be interested in mining.

Blithe, slightly tipsy, Henry squiggled inaccurately the Garonne and Dordogne rivers. He began, fortified by an additional swill of Margaux, an artistic shading of the Entre Deux Mers. One day he would go there, see for himself, at harvest-time. He saw himself stepping between vines, scrutinizing a bunch here, offering to the farmer a word of commendation (in local patois) there, this woman by his side. She'd not be in the tweeds, of course, elegant

as they were, she'd be in headscarf, he supposed, tailored slacks, something of that nature. Henry's imagina-
tion seized up. His knowledge of female dress was not
copious, but this side of the trip he could safely leave
to her, she would find something appropriate for wine-
harvesting. He would look after transport, hotel reser-
vations, documentation, administration, choice of restau-
rants, all of that.

'This really is a very great pleasure. Incidentally, my
name's Henry Butt.'

'Butt?' echoed Kate, marvelling.

This, though, was no moment for marvelling. Kate
swished her wine round her mouth. Was she now expected to give her own name? And would the voicing
of her name be to commit herself, an irrevocable step
towards a relationship? Almost all she possessed was her
name. To give it, exchange it, would be like, well, a
sort of surrender. A final swish, then she swallowed
down the wine.

'Miss Kennedy,' Kate said, head lowered.

'I beg your pardon?'

'Kennedy,' Kate blurted. Brian, glass-wiping behind
the bar, stared in her direction. Confused, she said,
'Katherine.'

'I don't want to speak out of turn, I only got in today,
from Toronto. Katherine.' Henry dared the name. He
had never known a Katherine. Come to that he had
never known a great number of girls : Mollys and Marys,
Louellas, Dorothys, Brendas, Berenices, Susans and Sallys,
he had never known any of these. Katherine had a decided ring. Katherine of Aragon. Katherine Hepburn.
'I was going to say, Katherine—'

'Kate.'

'Sorry?'

'Katherine sounds funny. You can call me Kate, if you like.'

'Are you sure?'

'It's quite all right.'

'What I was going to suggest, Kate, if you haven't had dinner, and I haven't, not yet, I don't know what the food's like here, but if you haven't eaten, that's to say, if you're not alone—'

'No.'

'Mm?'

'Not alone. Not exactly. I mean I wouldn't be sitting here alone, would I? Strange idea. I'm working. Yes. In a way.' Kate's speech galloped. 'Housekeeper. That's it. Staff. Business really.'

'You're the housekeeper?'

'Naturally. Not here, of course. Dublin. A new hotel. Very nice place. Very advanced. We're the same chain, you see. One of a chain. I'm on a reciprocal visit.'

Exhausted, Kate kept her mouth open and flung into it half a glassful of Margaux. The pink man—Butt, did he say?—was blinking at her through thick lenses. His mouth was opening and shutting, and from its interior issued words.

'That's fascinating. What I was about to say was, perhaps you might do me the honour of dining with me?'

'I will, thanks,' Kate said.

'If it's not too much trouble.'

'No. No, no. Not at all.'

Why should it be trouble? There was a tune in Kate's head which was not quite a tune, more a reverberation, like a plucked 'cello string. In her throat was something less agreeable, like a knot. *Wine is a mocker, strong drink is raging.* Kate's finger-tips flew to her lips, stifling a burp. *Who can find a virtuous woman? For her price is far above rubies.* Ah, it was true. And likely he'd pay in rubies for her supper, he was a Yankee all right with his talk and his fleecy jacket, he'd be rich as Croesus, like the rest of them. She'd have the chicken, if there was chicken. But gently with the tipple, Katie bawn, and Croesus beside her asking for another bottle like it was a birthday.

'Pomerol,' Henry was instructing Brian, stabbing at the wine list. 'Here, number twenty-four.'

Brian left, and the curly blinking pink man was saying, 'We can take it in with us, it should be opened before dinner, very good with game, any meat, cheese. Should we clean up first?'

'Clean up what?'

'What?'

'I'd best change my shoes,' Kate said, pushing her chair back.

'Me too,' said Henry. 'Back here in ten minutes, right?'

He allowed her to go first, pearl-grey and brushed black as tall as a twelve-year-old, threading in front of him through the Palm Room. At the door he mumbled confirmation of time and place which she did not hear as she trod off, click-clack click-clack, through the tiled lobby and up steps into carpeted acres and the hotel's

depths. Henry returned to Brian with instructions for
Pomerol temperature and breathing-time, then headed
for the lobby.

In the empty (he had believed) men's room he was
drying his face on a hand-towel when someone's forearm encircled his neck, his arms were gripped, and the
towel was pushed into his mouth.

As all that remained to Henry was his legs, he high-
jumped, and croaked in his throat like a frog as he high-
jumped, up and down, trying to bounce whoever was
on his back, off. In mid-bounce his legs were pulled
from under him. Henry had an impression of being
transported bodily through space. Then someone deton-
ated a bomb on top of his head.

CHAPTER V

Ramsey Gore, strutting through tussocky carpeting in
the direction of the lobby, slowed at the sound of the
elephant seal shedding its winter skin. The nearest elephant seal, he was sure, was in Phoenix Park Zoo,
Dublin.

'Urrrrrrgh!'

As Gore drew level with the passage to his left, he
marked time, watching the door to the men's room open,
and into the passage emerge knees, a torso, and finally
a head.

'Urrrrrrraaaaaagh!'

The Kilkelly Castle Hotel's owner and manager moved
seething into the passage. The figure from the men's

room, jacketless, trying to hook one end of its spectacles over an ear, was decorated with blood.

'What're you playing at, man! Get back in there—quick!' Ramsey Gore gestured towards the open door. 'Get in! You're not wandering about my hotel in that state!'

The figure hooked the gold-rimmed glasses successfully, smiled towards the sound of the manager's voice, and fell flat.

'Great sacred leaping creeping—get up, man!'

The figure stayed down, inert, bloodying the carpet.

Manager Gore was saying, 'He's all right. See him move? Playing the fool, that's about it. Skylarking. I'm giving him warning, he's not skylarking in my hotel.'

Henry opened his eyes. Obviously he was at the bottom of a swimming pool.

'Would you bring that American, the doctor?' another voice said. 'Isn't one of those golfers a doctor?'

'Doctor Langer,' said Gore. 'We don't need him. No sense broadcasting it. It's only a bruise.'

'Would you tell him anyway?'

'Fuss, fuss. Kiernan? Fetch that doctor. Bloody chiropodist, probably.'

A door opened, closed. Henry could make out two or three figures above him. He was not in a swimming pool. On a couch? They must have moved him. He felt comfortable, except for his head.

'Mr Butt?' said a face, closely peering. 'Can you talk?'

'No.'

'Don't talk. Don't worry at all. I'm going to ask you one or two questions, and you may answer by shaking or nodding your head. Tell me, who was it?'

Henry shook his head. A grave mistake.

'See? No one.' Gore, victorious. 'He slipped. Sloshed as a newt. Can't you smell the drink on him? Well, he's not staying in my hotel. Enough is enough.'

'Where are my glasses?' Henry said.

He tried sitting up. The headache intimated he would be better not trying, so he lay back again. Hands, not his own, placed the glasses on his nose.

'Inspector Mulligan,' said the man with the questions. He was tall, bald. Premature acomia, diagnosed Henry: no cure for it except a wig. 'This,' Inspector Mulligan said, 'is the manager, Mr Gore. Now, anything at all you can tell me, try, take it slowly, time could be vital.'

'Someone behind me. I didn't see him.'

'Nothing at all?'

'Nothing.'

'Hear anything?'

'No.'

'Surely you heard something?'

'Sorry.'

'Can I use your phone?'

'Go ahead.'

'Not you,' snarled Gore, and to the Inspector said, 'I'm going to start keeping an account. This is all very well.'

Henry saw blearily a third party, green and hovering, a flunkey. The door opened again, closed, men were arguing. Henry didn't bother to listen. Someone had removed his glasses again and he was being supported in a sitting position. Hands, headache, a wet warmth, furlongs of bandage, disinfectant smells.

'Is he all right?' the Inspector said.

'Depends what you mean by all right,' said an American voice.

Dr Langer, Henry surmised, the eminent golfing chiropodist. Though for a chiropodist he tied a tidy head-bandage. Henry watched a blur of tubby doctor unfurling shirtsleeves, buttoning cuffs. The hands closed a black medical bag like an attaché case.

'Merely a question of loss of blood, I'd say,' Gore said. 'Wouldn't you agree, Doctor?'

'Uh-hmm.'

'He fell against a tap.'

'Think so?'

'Drunk as a wheelbarrow. No need to gossip about it, what? I'm sure Mr Butt will settle your bill right away. That so, Butt? Hullo—Butt?'

'Who took my glasses'

By the time the glasses were restored and Henry had the world in focus, Dr Langer had gone. Gore, Mulligan and two entranced greenjackets remained. The room began to resemble an office. Inspector Mulligan was mumbling into a telephone.

'That doctor will cost you a pretty penny,' Gore told Henry. 'Don't think you'll get National Health rates from him. You realize he'll want dollars.'

Inspector Mulligan replaced the receiver. 'Would you mind leaving us for a few minutes'

'Me?' Gore looked from the Inspector to the casualty from the men's room, then back to the Inspector. He took from his pocket a bunch of keys, selected one, and ostentatiously locked the desk drawer. 'If that's how you feel. Kiernan? Brophy?' Gore strutted to the door. 'Any more of your phone calls, Inspector, I'd be grateful if you'd keep me informed.'

Alone with the policeman, Henry put his fingers to the tidy bandage.

'Why?' he said.

'That's the question,' said Mulligan.

'Where's my jacket?'

'This it?'

Henry felt in an inside pocket. He brought out pocket-book, passport, plastic folder of travellers' cheques, the McGrew letters. He said:

'That's something anyway. He didn't want these.'

'Or he didn't have time.'

'Oh?'

'Why,' Inspector Mulligan said, 'assault you, take nothing, then leave? Someone interrupted him.'

'Who?'

'Right. You're sure you saw nothing at all? Not a glimpse?'

'All I know is he's not happy about geologists.' Henry held out the McGrew letters. 'Have you seen these?'

'McGrew to his wife?'

'Yes.'

'We've copies.'

'Ah.'

'Of course, if he wasn't interrupted, it's possible he meant only to put the fear of God in you.'

'He succeeded.'

'I'll agree it's not much of a welcome to Ireland.'

'Well, he'll not succeed a second time.'

'No, we'll see to that.'

'I mean I'm not staying.'

'That might be wise.'

Henry's occiput expanded, contracted. When he man-
oeuvred his bulk fractionally sideways, the couch
creaked. 'But why? Harvey and McGrew vanish, but
I'm banged on the head.'

'Why?'

'I was asking you. It's inconsistent.'

''Tis a puzzler, I grant you.'

'If you find out, drop me a card. I'm vanishing too—
home.'

Zinc, lead, and whatever McGrew had thought he
had found, were not worth the candle. If he had thought
about it properly he would never have come. Let the
cops unravel it, that's what they were for, and when
they had settled it he would come back, and work.

'Toronto?' Mulligan said.

'You've done your homework.'

'We try to be prepared.'

A rapped tattoo on the door rocked Henry's skull
like an artillery barrage. He shut his eyes. When he
opened them Mulligan was listening to a uniformed
policeman with stripes on his sleeves and an open notebook in his hands.

The men's room, Henry gathered, had been photo-
graphed and fingerprinted.

Outside the window had been found indentations of
car tyres, though what with rain and the rough nature
of the gravel, these promised little.

All staff and guests had undergone preliminary questioning and of the thirty-one staff and seventeen guests
on the premises at the time of the assault, quoted Sergeant Byrne, turning notebook pages, the estimated
time being between seven-thirty and seven-forty p.m., fif-

teen staff and three guests could produce alibis showing
they had not been in or near the men's room . . .

Henry found the account sweetly soporific.

In the Palm Room at the time in question had been
the barman (Brian Mahoney), one American (William
N. Michelson), and one English bridge-player (Gertrude
Cowley). All others, it appeared, had suddenly wandered off to perfume themselves and change into eating-
clothes. One guest alone admitted to having entered
the men's room : the other English bridge-player.

'Cowley?' Mulligan said.

'Reginald Cowley,' said the Sergeant. 'Air Commodore, retired. He says he saw no one else there.'

'He must be eighty.'

'Seventy-three, sir. Stays here with his wife every
April, then on to the Spring Show in Dublin.'

'I know, I know. Did he hear or see anything in the
toilets?'

'I asked him if he glanced in the cubicles and he
replied, "Sergeant, be careful." '

'Phone Cork. Tell them we'd not say no to another
car.'

'Sir.'

'Not that phone, dammit. There's a coin-box by
Reception. And, Sergeant.'

'Sir?'

'There's a Super coming down from Dublin. Get your
notes in order.'

The closing door aroused Henry from a reverie of
scaloppini marsala at Old Angelo's, on Elm, four thousand miles away. And a pail of zabaglione to finish.

'I'm hungry,' said Henry, 'I think.'

'You ought to be in bed, Mr Butt,' Mulligan said. 'I'll have something brought up.'

'I've told you, I'm not staying in this place.'

'You'll be all right for tonight, sir. With respect, I think you're in no condition for travelling. I'll have one of my men keep an eye on you.'

CHAPTER VI

Inspector Mulligan not only allotted Henry a body-guard, he also moved him, and his baggage, into a different room.

Bathed, bandaged, pyjamaed, supine in bed waiting for something to eat, Henry heard discussions outside the door. The bodyguard, he deduced, was informing Ramsey Gore that the Inspector had moved the patient into a different room for security reasons; that for the same reasons no one had been told, not Mr Gore, or Reception, or anyone; and that now Mr Gore had found out, if he maundered about the place complaining and lamenting, God but the patient would likely have to be shifted again.

Henry listened to managerial oaths. Then peace. The wallpaper seemed familiar: overdressed cavaliers and maidens in bosky settings, surely the same that had papered the Palm Room, only there the papering had been roseate. Hadn't it? Here it was more kind of mulligatawny. There came a tap at the door. The door opened to admit the bodyguard's head and trunk. He was an eager young constable, farm-fed and muscled like a Kerry bull.

'Are yez all right, sor?'

'Thanks, hullo, I don't think I want anything to eat after all. I'm going to try to sleep.'

'Yez have been to sleep, sor. Yez oughta try and put the ham down. 'Twill give yez strength.'

Henry saw on the bedside table a tray with a plate of ham, bread rolls, cheese, fruit and a vacuum flask.

'What time is it?'

The constable stood in the doorway examining his watch. "Tis well on,' he said.

Though a competent quartermaster had issued the young buffalo with the most capacious uniform in stock, the seams strained. Horizontally across the chest, to left and right from each gasping button, rode creases in which a man could lose a finger.

'Where's my Pomerol?' Henry exclaimed, elbowing up into a sitting position and remembering, for the first time, Kate.

'Pomerwhat? A dog is it? She'll be around some-where, don't yez worry. Freedom, sor, they enjoy their freedom same as humans.'

Movement to the perpendicular had set up a jolting in Henry's head, but less severely, he decided, than before. 'Terrible,' he muttered. 'I'll have to explain.' He hooked on his glasses. Beside the tray he located his wristwatch. Twenty-nine minutes past midnight. Henry was aghast. The picture in his mind was of Kate Kennedy, visiting housekeeper, alone in the empty umbrageous Palm Room, waiting for her date. 'I have to go to the Palm Room,' Henry said, standing and looking round for clothing.

'Pardon, sor, but I'd say if that's the bar on the right as you come in, she'd not be allowed in there.'

'What?' inquired Henry, discovering a fallen shirt. On the collar was an unattractive russet stain. He lifted a suitcase onto the bed. Where were his pants, keys? She couldn't still be waiting. How long had she waited? Had anyone told her what had happened? He tried to remember the interview with the cop. Mulligan, was it? Hadn't everyone in the hotel been questioned? She had surely been told. Or had they been questioned but not told? What must she think of him? He said, 'Has everyone been told?'

''Tis a possibility.' The bodyguard was thoughtful. He took a pace into the room and pushed the door shut. The ditches in his tunic creaked and strained. 'But I'd say 'tis on the early side yet. She could be with the housekeeper.'

'True,' agreed Henry. Housekeepers would cling together, fretting about staff problems, the rising cost of floor polish. Gingerly he pulled a clean shirt over his head.

'Or the hall porter.'

'I don't see,' Henry mumbled, turbaned head surfacing, 'why she'd be with the hall porter.'

''Twould be the night porter. If the day porter had her first, he might pass her on to the night porter.'

Henry blinked at the bodyguard. Thinking before speaking, he said, 'Do you know her?'

'Not personally, sor, I've not had that pleasure, but I've a fondness for them. My brother has one. A bitch. Ears like arrowheads, so she has. Sometimes I take her out meself, Sundays, when there's no hurley. I give her a bit of a runaround.'

Frowning, Henry stepped into trousers. He had never enjoyed this kind of talk. The bodyguard took out a murky handkerchief and blew his nose.

'Is yours a bitch, did y' say, sor?'

'I'd appreciate it, officer, if we discussed something else. Perhaps you'd return to your duty.'

'No worry, sor, no one will slide past me. If yez is thinking of seeking the porter I'll accompany yez. 'Tis orders. Did yez say Pomeralium? I've heard of them. Are they the foxy-faced divils? The ones with the pointy snout?'

The bodyguard never had a chance to discover. At this instant the door flew open and into his back. Instead of being everlastingly crippled by the impact he whirled, a blur of blue uniform, fists like watermelons raised for action. Simultaneously he emitted a banshee wail.

'Aweeeeeeegh!'

The wail, designed to demoralize, pierced Henry like a needle. He sat with a jolt, trembling, on the edge of the bed. Men were coming into his bedroom.

'Mother of God, will you gi' ower that!' Inspector Mulligan edged past the bodyguard. 'You're supposed to be in the corridor.'

The bodyguard lowered the watermelons. Mulligan advanced on Henry with the suffering expression of a football coach who has interrupted his star forward experimenting with pot.

'With respect, Mr Butt, you'd be as well in bed, there are no planes tonight. I'd like you to meet Superintendent O'Malley.'

A step behind the Inspector came a square, grey man

wearing a grey raincoat and a trampled hat. His eyes were grey, fringed by grey spiky eyebrows like parched grass. He held out his hand. Over the Superintendent's shoulder, half in hiding behind the bodyguard, Henry spied Ramsey Gore in blazer and cravat.

'Pleased to meet you, Mr Butt,' said the Superintendent. 'Sorry about the circumstances. How's the head?'

'Middling.'

'You should rest it, you shouldn't be up. Are you away already?' The grey man eyed the suitcases. 'I thought you were staying the night.'

'Mr Butt is anxious about his dog, sor,' the bodyguard said.

'Dog?'

'A Pomeralium, sor. We were off to consult with the night porter.'

'Couldn't you phone down? Mr Butt shouldn't be running about the place.'

'We weren't going to run, sor, we were going to move steady. Mr Butt hasn't eaten his ham.'

'Why not?' Superintendent O'Malley looked darkly at the ham. 'Is it salty?'

"Tis grand ham, sor. 'Tis the Galtee.'

'You'll find no finer ham than this,' Ramsey Gore announced, advancing. He stooped scrutinizing the ham, straightened up, smirked. 'Of course, after the seventh Martini the American palate is hardly a fit judge.'

'Canadian,' Henry said, and having had enough of Gore, added, 'Buster.'

'What?' Gore said.

'It wasn't Martini either. It was Margaux.'

'Raving,' said Gore.

'While we're setting the record straight, I haven't got a dog.' Sitting on the bed's edge, Henry looked at Mulligan. 'I suppose you wouldn't know, is there a lady left in the Palm Room?'

The policemen exchanged glances.

'What sort,' Mulligan inquired, 'of a lady?'

'Miss Kennedy. We were going to dine together.'

'Restaurant's closed,' Gore said, 'so you can put that idea out of your head.'

'Mr Gore,' said Inspector Mulligan, smiling like a hangman, 'perhaps you could leave us now. Thank you for your assistance.'

'If you move him again,' Gore said, 'use the same sheets. This isn't a charitable institution.'

The manager, glowering, made an ungracious exit. At a nod from the Inspector the bodyguard returned to the corridor and shut the door. O'Malley dragged a chair towards the bed, established it beside the bedside table, and sat.

'I'll be frank, Mr Butt. We haven't got to the bottom of this. But we will. I understand there's not much you can tell us.'

'Afraid not,' said Henry.

'But you're thinking of returning to Toronto.'

'Wouldn't you?'

'What will happen to the assays—assaying? Is that the word? The analyzing, at Carrigann. Will someone take your place?'

'If they're lunatic enough they might. Depends on the president.'

'Ogden.' The Superintendent, swivelling, helped himself to a slice of ham. 'Zinc and lead, is that right?'

'Apparently. Look—'

'These other two, Harvey and McGrew, your predecessors, did you know them at all?'

'Not well.'

'What can you tell me? I never knew either.'

'McGrew was very able.' Was? Henry stroked his bandage. 'Harvey's reckoned a trifle academic, he did a controversial paper on the reactives—potassium, sodium.'

'Stable, would you say? I mean, not likely to hop off with the wage packets? Or a girl?'

'I really couldn't tell you. Wouldn't have thought so.'

'And zinc and lead, the stuff you've found at Carrigann, they're very commercial?' Superintendent O'Malley parted a piece of ham with his fingers and tucked the larger part into his mouth. 'What I'm saying is, there's money in it?'

'If there's enough, and you can get it out, and once you've got it out you can get it away. It costs money. Look, officer, I wonder—'

'Silver would be the more precious,' said the Superintendent, buttering a roll. 'There'd be a profit in that? Or gold?'

'There's no gold at Carrigann. You're carboniferous. Grits and limestones and shales.'

'Turf.'

'What?'

'Peat,' explained the Superintendent, licking at a crumb. 'But Carrigann's practically in the Galtee, wouldn't you say?'

'Pardon?'

'Galtee?' Henry felt the thread of the conversation was rapidly being drawn away from him. 'The ham?'

'The Galtee Mountains. They're igneous. Granites and basalts, isn't that right? Might you not find gold there?'

'Possibly,' Henry admitted, startled and cautious, his professional reputation suddenly at hazard. Had the policeman been given a fast briefing or was he genuinely knowledgeable?

Inspector Mulligan, Henry noticed, stood watching his chief in admiration.

'I can't help you when I've not even seen the place,' Henry said, stretching towards the suitcase. He burrowed for a tie. The sober navy one with the diamond shapes. If she was still waiting he would at least be correctly dressed. 'There might be silver. You've seen McGrew's letter, presumably. He seems to have thought he was on to something. But you don't just dig and haul up crates of bullion, you realize that. Anyone who goes about kidnapping and mugging people who may have struck silver is uneducated.'

'There are educated knaves, and uneducated. Platinum?' Superintendent O'Malley chewed. 'Isn't platinum the most precious metal?'

'Yes, quite valuable, depending on the markets, but this is Ireland. Not Canada, or South Africa.' Henry stood up. 'If you'll excuse me, I must try and get hold of Miss Kennedy. She may well have given up. I'll phone down—'

'Ireland,' O'Malley said, 'has knaves enough, God bless us, but they're in a small way, most of 'em. You know what I mean, Mr Butt. Two tellys and a transistor missing from the corner shop, a bag of cement from the builders' yard. Ructions at closing-time with the fists flapping like laundry in a wind. Faulty brakes on the family limousine. I'm not sayin' 'tis all the small time. We have our moments.' The Superintendent licked his buttery fingers. 'F'rinstance now, there are some fair old arsenals tucked away. We've weaponry enough in kitchen cupboards to equip a regiment. But that's not crime, that's political. I'm fancying this isn't political. This is big business. Shall I tell you a dream I had?'

Henry, dressed, chafing, set to go, to beard the dark Irish Kennedy in the darkened Palm Room, opened his mouth cautiously.

'I dreamed,' O'Malley said, 'a bright boardroom.'

Henry, mouth open, nodded. The Superintendent had unscrewed the cup from the flask and was pouring coffee.

'What you fellas might call an executive suite, gaudy with light. I'll be honest, I guessed 'twas the cabinet at Leinster House. We've an election coming up.'

'I see,' said Henry, and sat down.

'Superintendent O'Malley has dreams,' Mulligan said.

'It might have been the cabinet and it might not. It might have been somewhere foreign, like your Ivernia lads in Toronto. Or it might have been—' the Superintendent blew on his coffee. He appeared to be in a waking dream, voice hushed, eyes fixed on the bosky papering on the far side of the room—'it might have been your County Leitrim Machine-Knitters and Hosiery Limited. That's the trouble with dreams.'

'What is?' Henry said.

'They defy analysis.'

'Superintendent O'Malley has had several outstanding successes,' Mulligan said.

'Good,' Henry said, 'good.' The subject was clearly so charged with importance that he hesitated to change it, but he said, 'Excellent. Amazing. I'll just find out about Miss Kennedy, then this flight reservation, and I'll cable my boss in Toronto.'

'We've sent a telegram to your Mr Ogden,' Inspector Mulligan said. 'And you've no worry about Miss Kennedy. She's gone.'

'Gone?'

'Don't vex yourself about your dog either,' O'Malley said. 'We'll have the rascal back by morning.'

'You're sure it was Miss Kennedy—Katherine Kennedy?' Henry asked the Inspector.

'About nine, in a taxi. Paid her account and left.'

'Oh,' said Henry, and after a pause, 'Oh, well.'

CHAPTER VII

Garda Griffin, farm-fed bodyguard, steered the garda car along a serpentine detour towards Carrigann.

Sunshine bounced upon the car's black bonnet. A breeze brushed and swayed the banked grass on either side of the road. In the hedgerows early fuschia swung like drips of blood. Over the tops of the hedgerows and through gaps left by farm gates, farmland browns and greens and yellows sped past. The detour grew ever more complex. Garda Griffin said:

'There's a passage left is a short cut, sor, I know her well enough, only I don't know as I'd recommend it after the rain. We could get bogged in.'

'Keep straight on,' said Inspector Mulligan in the front passenger seat.

In the back, Superintendent O'Malley said, "Tis a powerful day. We've time to play with. Will there be anything to see?"

'Can't say,' Henry said. 'Boreholes?'

'Grand, grand.' O'Malley massaged his hands, watching through the window the April day. The countryside lifted in greeting, then shied away, a diminishing, undulating prospect of pasture and meadow, warped and buckled like a gramophone record left in the sun. 'I've never seen a borehole.'

One borehole, Henry could have told him, was much like another. He felt not in the least cheerful. The sensation within his turbaned skull reminded him of student hangovers.

In the car's trunk were his cases. His flight reservation was for 18.00 hours. He was in retreat. The O'Malley Plan was for a leisurely survey of the Carrigann site, which neither had seen; leisurely lunch; leisurely drive to Shannon Airport; and goodbye, Ireland, Mr O'Malley, goodbye, Mr Butt, sorry about everything, everyone, God bless, 'bye Inspector, so sorry. One day in Ireland, one day and a bit, with nothing accomplished: would this, Henry wondered, be a record? A pity, now that the sun was shining. Distantly a slate-roofed farmhouse with television mast came into view, obliterated in the next instant by a surge of hedge. On the other side of the hedge, motionless in a field, sprawled pensive cows, monolithic pottery ornaments in the sun. A pointless, senseless trip, and a pity.

But to stay, a morsel for an unidentified geologist-eater, would be more senseless. Better retreat and live than stay and vanish. Henry opened his snuff tin, parked a hill of powder on his thumbnail, lifted it to his nose, and sniffed. He sneezed ferociously.

'I'd always been led to understand,' said O'Malley, 'that you weren't supposed to sneeze with that stuff. Isn't that the point, part of the ritual and all, not to sneeze?'

'I always sneeze,' Henry said, and he hiked up his glasses so that he could dab at wet eyes.

'There it is, down there, Carrigann,' said the Inspector.

In the back seat the Superintendent and Henry leaned and looked. Garda Griffin cornered and momentarily a thicket of roadside elms obscured the view. Then the car once more dipped towards Carrigann: a pair of intersecting streets, a church, houses and shops painted by an extrovert with access to too many colours, tractors assembled at the petrol pump, a war memorial, dogs, parked cars. A sun-warmed relic, a stone survival in a green world. The cuisine won't be five-star, I'm well out of it, Henry told himself, trying to suppress a regret.

The bodyguard steered across a bridge over a river and into the village. Along both sides of both streets cars were parked. To Superintendent O'Malley the scene was frisky enough to be a Sunday, Mass just concluded. Knots of men disputed and shared opinions. Alone or in groups, with evident purposefulness, others strode the pavements, criss-crossed the road.

'Boom town,' O'Malley murmured.

'Where to now, sor?' requested Griffin.

'Keep on slowly, lad, the five-dollar tour,' O'Malley said.

'She's a boom town now all right, but you should have seen her a couple of months ago, empty as a navvy's glass.' Inspector Mulligan wound down his window, the better to survey the boom. 'See those boyos, over there, none of 'em are local.'

'Who are they then?' O'Malley wanted to know.

'Stockbrokers, I dare say, come to see for themselves. Middlemen, share-pushers, scroungers, chancers, newshounds with nothing better to do. We've all sorts and conditions in Carrigann. It was busier than this when Harvey was here, and McGrew, and the results were coming in, but half of them left when the drilling stopped. There's been no drilling since Mr Harvey disappeared. They'll be back, I expect.'

'Why?' O'Malley said.

Inspector Mulligan, watching through the window, fingered an earlobe. He had invested a hundred pounds of his own savings in Ivernia. 'Curiosity, profit, wanting to be where it's happening. You'd be amazed. I've met some who thought they were going to con Paddy Boland into selling them an acre. Then with each new announcement of more lead and more zinc they're chasing round in circles. Most of the time they don't know whether they ought to be selling their shares or buying more.'

'That one, there, he could be a Yank, wouldn't you say?' O'Malley said.

'We'll stop, he might be with Ivernia,' said Mulligan. 'Mr Butt can have a chat.'

'No, no, keep going,' Henry said. 'I don't know him.'

Compatriots questioning about his head, who he was, so who'd replace him if he was quitting no sooner than he'd arrived, and wasn't it tough that progress should be held up for lack of a geologist just when Carrigann's potential was beginning to look starry? Henry needed none of that. So far as he was aware no one from Ivernia was in Carrigann other than himself, not at this early stage. Time enough for the technicians and administrators when the assaying was done and a decision had been made to pull the stuff out of the ground.

The garda car gathered speed. 'That looks like Ivernia,' Henry said, gazing through the window at machinery.

Bodyguard Griffin had left Boom Town as abruptly as he had entered it. In the field to the left a drilling-rig spiked up into the air: a tripod of steel tubing twenty-five feet high. No drilling was in progress. No one occupied the lorry, buried to its axles in waving grass. The corrugated-iron shed which had been set up at the field's edge was deserted. The site wore a desolate abandoned air. Without a company geologist on the spot to differentiate between zinc and worthless rock and to decide the positioning of the next borehole, work had ceased. Action, with the vanishing of Harvey, had ground to a muddy halt. Dermot Reaney, Jack Sheehan, the O'Rourke brothers, Tim Kavanagh, all the hired local labour from Mallow, Buttevant, Doneraile, from Carrigann itself, had been paid off and sent home, back to the farms and roads, to await word that drilling was on again. Billy Devlin, foreman, had motored home to Cork and his self-made business, seeking and drilling for water for the rich immigrants in mansions remote from the mains. Mrs Devlin knitted near the telephone, awaiting official word from Toronto that a replacement for

Mr Harvey had arrived, and was set.

Inspector Mulligan motioned the bodyguard-driver to take a turning to the right. The garda car bundled up a boreen between fields. 'Here's your Ivernia lot, too,' Mulligan said. 'They were drilling here up to last week.'

'I can see,' Henry said, looking out at another unmanned rig.

A stepladder had been left propped against a leg of the tripod. Planks, an iron bar, a shovel, lay on the ground near the borehole. There was a pile of concrete blocks.

'Disappointing,' O'Malley said. ''Tis unspectacular. Can I not see drilling?'

First deliver us from evil, then you can see drilling, Henry wanted to say. He said, 'There's only the din of the drill, nothing to look at.'

'I'd pictured explosions and the rock whizzing every way.'

'The rock whizzes, splinters of it. But no explosions.'

'Well, 'tis all a bit derelict and disappointing. Queer to think this land might become worth something.'

'I'd guess the value's about quadrupled,' Henry said, 'since Ivernia moved in.'

'When prices go up that swift, all I know is, it's a headache for some.'

'You're talking to the expert,' Henry murmured.

Pink and large, leaning his forehead against the cold of the window, Henry gazed upon Ivernia's licensed tracts of green. 'There was a drill smashed somewhere. Could we see that?'

Inspector Mulligan looked at his watch. 'It's two

miles north and nothing when you get there. They've taken the drill. If you like we can, but we'd be getting off the track.'

'Doesn't matter then,' Henry said.

'Next left back to Carrigann,' Mulligan told the driver.

The sun had given up, leaving in the sky a grubby menace. Bodyguard Griffin circled the car round a field bearing a third drill. What, wondered Henry, had McGrew thought he had found?

'I'd say we're lucky it's no worse than a headache,' the Superintendent said. 'The best sense is there were two of them at least. They wanted you away out of it. They knew you were at Kilkelly, they expected you, and the first chance you gave them, they banged you.'

The trio sat on a bench by a window in Egan's: Henry and the two garda detectives. Henry and Superintendent O'Malley held pint glasses of stout. Inspector Mulligan, a Pioneer, drank a Fanta orange. Griffin was absent; waiting in the garda car, Henry supposed, or eating sandwiches under a tree.

'Why they banged you, I don't know yet,' O'Malley admitted. 'McGrew sounds to me as though he thought he'd got something. So that might be why they disposed of him. When Harvey arrived they had to dispose of Harvey, in case. When you arrived, Mr Butt, they tried to dispose of you. I'd be interested to know if there's something under the crust besides lead and zinc. What about the radioactive stuff—uranium?'

Henry shook his head.

'What we want,' O'Malley said, 'is more drilling and a geologist.'

Wonderingly, not unappreciative, Henry sipped the

weird black stout : bitter and soupy. Through the window he watched noontime in Carrigann. Since the day, now part of history, when McGrew had described the village as one-horse, with no special reason for existence, change had overhauled the community. The two streets simmered with intruders and their cars. Rival pubs were enjoying business as boozily lucrative as Egan's. Never mind the bickering of tractors, the gas pump was dry again, and an ale-flushed farmer with a screwdriver was scratching an opinion into its paint. Discarded copies of the *Wall Street Journal* and the *Financial Times* had accumulated in the lidless bin outside the post office. Billy Dunne polished with a handkerchief the headlights of his taxi. With a peaked cap, licence, and a heavy middle-aged saloon car, he had entered the taxi business four weeks earlier, convinced there was loot to be had in the ferrying about of the big pots, now fame had come to Carrigann. Originally black, his car was now a charred shade, as though at some stage it might have been involved in a fire. Proprietor Dunne had painted the mudguards bright yellow, and with the same paint inscribed along each side, *Dunne's Taxicab Service. Weddings & Private Entertainments Catered For. Prop. W. Dunne. Tel. Carrigann 57.*

Word of a possible bonanza (for the developer and shareholders) at Carrigann had gone forth and brought in the curious and the committed : journalists, stock-brokers, spies from Ivernia competitors, tradesmen, rural conservationists, industrialists and contractors with an eye on development, politicians with an eye on votes.

'One of them waited in a car outside the men's room window while the other clubbed you, the intention being defenestration, and exit geologist in car.' Superintendent O'Malley took a long pull of stout. 'But Air Commodore Cowley arrived. He says he saw nothing, which I believe, so probably your knave had dragged his unconscious geologist into a toilet and hid there. Until Cowley had gone.' Once more a deep swallow, the gasp of satisfaction. 'By the time Cowley had gone, perhaps the car had gone too. Or why not continue the defenestration?'

'I don't know,' Henry said. 'Why not?'

'I'm asking. 'Tis what we term a loose end. All of this is theory. If you weren't the successor to Harvey and McGrew, no offence now, but I might even have paid heed to that manager fellow's theory.'

'That I was drunk?'

'Something like that. You'd had the one bottle of wine, was that it?'

'Shared it,' Henry amended, idly looking for and failing to find wine-drinkers among the Egan's throng.

Egan's was socially less elevated than the Palm Room but better populated, snugger, and the conversation of higher quality. A score of men stood at the counter and in the centre of the room. Others, local and imported, sat on benches round the walls. The locals discussed anthrax, the barley harvest, next Sunday's hunt, hurley, rising prices; the immigrants, share prices and the world recession in zinc. Both groups, glancing towards the plainclothes policemen and bandaged Henry, examined in low voices those rumours from Kilkelly of the latest geologist-battering. A coal fire burned in the grate, and from behind the bar would advance, from time to time, Egan's daughter, or Egan himself, to stir the embers and feed fresh black cobs into the glow. As no one read, wrote, played darts (there were no darts), or did anything except drink, ponder and talk, no one, particularly Egan, had thought to turn on the lights, and the room was crepuscular, fire and window being the only sources of light. The floor was bare boards, the smell spirits and stout, tobacco and coal-smoke.

'I shared it,' said Henry, staring through the window, and pointing, 'with her. Look, there, that's her. Pardon me a moment.'

Henry elbowed through the mob and into the dazzle of the street.

'Kate!' he called, waving. 'Hullo there—Miss Kennedy!'

She was walking away from him, on the opposite side of the street, and if she heard she gave no sign. She wore the same grey tweed and carried a handbag. Henry hurried in pursuit. By the time he had caught up he was round the corner. Already they seemed to have left behind Main Street, Carrigann. The road ribboned forward into countryside.

'Hullo, how do you do? Miss Kennedy?'

Her eyes failed to ignite with pleasure. She did not slow her pace. 'It's you,' she said.

'Yes, it is,' said Henry, eager, loping alongside.

Over the next hundred yards he narrated the previous evening's mishap. He was beginning to think he detected a softening when he glanced back towards the crescendo of a car engine.

The car, chlorophyll-green and sporty with gross, switchback mudguards and flatulent exhausts, was accelerating towards them. Because a passenger was leaning from a window, aiming a gun, Henry tried to dodge

through an opening : a pair of stone gateless pillars in a
high wall of which he had time for only the haziest impression. He blundered into Miss Kennedy, realizing
too late that unless he moved away from her fast, she too
might be hurt. They were both falling, groping at each
other for support, when the car passed and the gun
exploded.

'I'm shot,' complained Kate, earthbound, in a tiny
voice.

CHAPTER VIII

'Where?' Henry cried.

'Mmmmm,' moaned the tiny voice.

They sprawled, Miss Kennedy and Mr Butt, in the
opening in the high wall. The ground was granite chip-
pings, mud, a shrivelled apple core. Henry's flank and
palms were grazed and tingling, his glasses askew. Kate
moaned the small moan, and it frightened her, seeming
to come from far off.

Her pain was generalized : head, back, legs. She was
alive, she realized, but for how much longer? All she
could see was blue sky. Her fingers scrabbled through
gravel for her handbag, her brain boiled with questions.
My handbag? Am I dying? My skirt, is it up or down?
Is it tights or stockings I'm wearing today? Blessed
Mary full of grace if I'm dying forgive me my sins as
we forgive them that sin against us and lead us not into
temptation, let me be wearing tights, should I speak
aloud, try to, my last words, what are my dying words?

Mmmmmmm. Where's that terrible man? Praise God I'm wearing tights am I not? What's happening? Where's my handbag?

'Stand back, please, mind now,' a voice of authority was saying.

'I saw it, he charged her down,' said a woman. 'Watch him, the big fella with the bandage, he has a pistol.'

''Twas someone,' a man said, 'in the car had the pistol, yer lardy great blind-eyes.'

'Ah, go haunt yerself!'

'Give 'em a smoke, who's got smokes?'

'He barged her down, I saw it. Someone phone Dr Riley.'

'Dr Riley's away in Cork. 'Tis his day off.'

'A good job. Riley's a butcher.'

'I've smokes meself, y'see, but they're tipped. I can't take 'em plain. 'Tis the tips sop up the mortal ingredients.'

'Move on, shift y'selves,' the voice of authority said.

'Inspector,' said Henry from the ground, glimpsing through the press of legs the garda car. Late but resolute, Inspector Mulligan stooped over the fallen pair. Missing bodyguard at the wheel, Superintendent O'Malley beside him, the car moved off in pursuit of the green sports car. 'Inspector—an ambulance. Miss Kennedy's been shot.'

'Easy now, don't talk, don't worry at all,' Inspector Mulligan said.

Henry, sure he had somewhere received these instructions before, discovered that he was kneeling. A meagre little man in a cap was kneeling beside him, offering a cigarette.

'No, thank you,' Henry said, and turned to his fallen comrade. 'Miss Kennedy, please, it's all right, don't talk.'

'I wasn't going to, not to you.'

Testy, pale, Miss Kennedy sat upright. She seized her handbag and jerked the tweed skirt down to her knees. One leg was bent under her, out of sight. She lifted herself, unfolded the leg into view, and sat again. The foot was shoeless and bleeding. Kate stared at it in horror. 'I told you!' she said.

'Thank God,' Henry announced.

'Thank God?' Kate glared. 'Aren't I shot? And who's to blame? You did it! But for you I'd be sitting having my lunch.'

'I don't think that's quite fair. What—'

'Go away!'

'Miss, here, have a smoke,' said the little man in the cap, holding the cigarette to Kate's lips.

Kate pushed aside hand and cigarette. Her head and shoulders she thrust forward at Henry. 'You're a man of violence!'

'I'm not, really. No, you're wrong.'

'Yes, you are. Look at your head.'

'That's not my fault. I didn't do it.'

'I've no ankle!' Kate's anger was gone, swamped in sobs. 'They've shot off my ankle!'

'No, no, not off, truly,' assured Henry, leaning forward, comforting. 'I mean, you can see. If you look. Look. It's all there. Just a nick. Dab of disinfectant—'

'You did it, I know you did, you shot me!'

Kate sobbed and shook. A crowd a dozen strong and increasing pressed round. Henry gaped up at the faces for friends: some faces were sympathetic, some hostile.

'What did I say?' said a woman, triumphant.

'Get rid o' the gun, boy, quick,' a sympathetic face whispered down. 'Give it here.'

'Nonsense,' Henry muttered, standing up. 'She's upset. We're all upset.'

He brushed gravel from his trousers. The opening in the wall was a gateway without gates, the beginning of an unkempt, cratered drive leading to an even less kempt but grandiose house a hundred paces away. On one of the gateway's stone pillars, in recent paint, was the information : CARRIGANN PARK HOTEL. SELECT ACCOMMODATION. Down the drive towards the scene of the accident hastened two select staff.

The scene of the accident was confused. The little man in the cap had set fire to the filter tip of his cigarette and was puffing hard at the wrong end. Inspector Mulligan, harrowed by the collapsed woman's vapours, played for time. 'Move on there, I'm a guard and I'd like you to keep moving.' He moved among the crowd. 'It's all over, nothing to see, no obstructing the thoroughfare please.' No one heeded him except a girl who presented a shoe. 'What's this?' Inspector Mulligan said.

"Tis hers I'm sure, look, it matches her other. It was on the ground.'

'Right, thanks.'

'Will it be an exhibit?'

'Never you mind.' The Inspector circled the perimeter of the concourse, bald head in slow, burnished orbit. 'Keep moving there, back to the pubs, move along please.' A breathless young guard, traces of cabbage on his lower lip, saluted and was told, 'About time, see to the casualty, name's Kennedy, Miss Kennedy, and get statements from anyone who saw anything. I'll control the crowd.'

Rescued, immensely cheered, the Inspector turned his back on breathless Garda Feeney and swaying, sobbing Kate and moved like a programme-seller into the spectators. 'Back to your homes, the party's over,' he exhorted, starting to enjoy himself, and remembering in a burst of nostalgia his own salad days as a uniformed guard, the crowd-control sessions during visits of foreign potentates: President de Gaulle, two Yankee Presidents, a popular Mayor of West Berlin, a burnoused sheik, and those successions of Catholic tyrants, some white, some black, from crushed but sunny republics. 'Move along there,' Inspector Mulligan, called out, vaguely gesturing with the shoe.

Henry hovered over Kate. 'We must get the ambulance,' he told the uniformed guard.

'I know what we must do,' lied Garda Feeney, 'and I'll thank you not to interfere.'

'Don't offer her smokes,' said the man in the cap, inhaling like a suction pump. 'She's a non-smoker.'

'God save us, 'tis Miss Kennedy, she's with us,' said one of the pair who had hurried down the drive. 'What's it about then? Are ye all right, ma'am?'

'Stayin' with you, is she, Cooney?' asked Garda Feeney, whose local reputation was that of a busybody.

'I said so,' Cooney said. 'Arrived last night, we gave her the salmon.'

'Salmon,' Cooney's partner said.

'Bring up transport then,' said Garda Feeney. 'She's best at your place.'

'What's goin' on? Is it the foot, Miss Kennedy?'

'Don't be wastin' all day chattin',' Garda Feeney said.

'Get on with it.'

'Get on wi' what?'

'Transport. I have to take statements.'

'Will we need,' said Cooney, 'stretcher-bearers?'

'Stretcher-bearers,' said the partner.

'That's a point.' Garda Feeney adjusted his peaked cap, stooped, and addressed the woman in a bedside voice. 'Can ye walk, ma'am?'

'Of course I can't walk!' Kate dug in her handbag for a tissue. 'I'm shot in the ankle!'

'If someone,' said Henry, 'will just say where's the nearest phone, I'll get an ambulance.'

'Keep outa this, I'll brook no interference,' Garda Feeney said. He unbuttoned his breast pocket. 'In fact, I'll have your name for a start.'

'Get it from Mr Mulligan,' Henry said. 'Or you could ask the Superintendent when he gets back.'

'Yes, all right then. You can see the conditions, sir, it do be a matter of co-operation, I'm sure you'll agree, sir.' Brushing cabbage from his lip, Garda Feeney turned back to the casualty. 'Now, ma'am, if these gentlemen and me supported you decently, could you hop a bit? 'Tis no distance up the drive.'

'We could make a chair like for sportin' heroes,' Cooney suggested.

'Sportin' heroes and sportin' heroines,' said the partner.

Partner Flynn had the shine and stature of a Victoria plum, carmine-coloured, and topped by a plastered finger of hair like a stalk. Figuratively and physically he looked up to the younger Cooney. Cooney, an unsmiling, bending banana of a man, was the partnership's dynamo, chugging but steady. His polished suit hung

like distress signals on a becalmed freighter. Cooney
and Flynn, cousins, were still short of many items of
standard hotel equipment, including hotelier's clothing.
They had been hoteliers for five weeks, since noting the
influx of visitors to Carrigann. They had led the greyhounds and some incapable elderly relatives down to the
echoing basement, and from the remaining three storeys
were now prospering as never before.

'A chair?' Garda Feeney said. 'I'd been considerin'
that. You mean a chair like with hands and wrists?'

'Right so,' said Cooney, 'and a folded jacket or
blanket, something decent like that, for cushioning.'

'What cushioning?'

"Tis more suitable for a lady if there's a folded jacket.'

'If you could just lever y'self up, ma'am.' Bedside
alchemy pulsing in his voice, Garda Feeney bent towards Kate. 'No, your hand on my arm, ma'am, there,
'tis a matter of transferrin' you to a place of refuge,
don't y' see? That's it now. Fine. Cooney, Flynn, make
the chair.'

Cooney and Flynn, co-proprietors of the Carrigann
Park Hotel, made not so much a chair as a chaise-longue,
or more precisely a rickshaw, without wheels, but with
Flynn's ample ribcage as back-rest. Aided by the guard,
Kate was lowering herself backwards towards the rickshaw's interlocked wrists and forearms when Cooney
cried, 'Halt! We've forgotten the folded jacket,' whereupon the rickshaw dissolved and Kate was left frozen
in a sitting posture, wounded foot a-dangle. Garda
Feeney, holding her elbows, breathed rapidly and turned
his eyes to the ground. Never before had he been in
such proximity to a woman, other than his mother. 'That

should do it,' Cooney said, nodding as Flynn folded his jacket into a cushion.

Cushioned, the rickshaw became a woolsack, an upholstered tumbril, wheel-less but mobile, and collapsible. 'Wait now,' Flynn said. 'My wrist is cracking. We've lost the grip.'

Cooney said, 'Your left hand over my right. One of you take off the cushion so we can see.'

Henry lifted the jacket, Flynn and Cooney interspliced wrists and forearms. 'That's not it, we're a mile off,' Cooney said. 'How was it before?'

They pondered, relinked, under and over, and withdrew. They attempted a trellis pattern, over, through and round. Next, a reticulated meshwork of hands and arms which, Henry pointed out, would not do because at no point were they holding each other, at every point they were holding themselves. Puzzled, gripping their own hands and wrists, the co-proprietors stepped apart, and the semblance of a chair disappeared. They stepped together, interweaved from a new angle, and Cooney said, 'Is that it?'

Henry said, 'Does anyone remember the Fireman's Lift?'

Kate began to sob.

'Ah no,' said Garda Feeney, clutching Kate's elbows and looking at the sky. 'No, no, no, no.'

'Chair lift, is it? Grand, grand, keep it up,' called out Inspector Mulligan, drawing near. He moved away on a fresh circuit of crowd dispersal. 'Move on, please, no obstructing the highway.'

'Aisy back, Miss,' coaxed Cooney. 'Aisy now. Over a bit. Whoops! Aisy.'

Kate reversed precariously onto the folded jacket. Flynn's carpal bones creaked. The proprietors had failed to reconstitute the original rickshaw but they had achieved a passable jaunting-car. Kate clung to lapels and biceps. Garda Feeney clasped Kate's elbows and focused his gaze upwards on a feather of cirrus. Henry posted himself as backstop. The cavalcade moved off with a lurch.

They achieved a spanking pace. Dust and gravel spurted. In obedience to shouts from Cooney, a car journeying from the hotel steered into the pasture and sank upto its hubcaps, leaving a clear passage along the rocky driveway. A moment after the casualty party had vanished into the hotel, the garda car returned. Bodyguard Griffin parked at the stone pillars.

'John,' Superintendent O'Malley called through the window.

Inspector Mulligan ran to the car. 'No luck?' he inquired.

'We've got a corpse,' said the Superintendent. 'Where's Butt?'

CHAPTER IX

'Harvey,' said Henry.

'Not McGrew, you're sure,' said O'Malley.

'Harvey.'

'It's not good enough, John.' O'Malley grimaced in the direction of Inspector Mulligan. 'I thought the first thing you did was search the hotel.'

'I'll speak to Sergeant Byrne.' Mulligan, gruff, evaded responsibility. 'The rooms in this turret have been locked since October, all of them. I told Byrne to get a pass-key.'

'Can we go now?' said Henry. He was holding a handkerchief to his nose.

'Not yet,' O'Malley said. 'You can open the window.'

'I will,' Henry said, and did so. He stayed at the window, head out, looking down on the lake and golf course.

'Phew,' blew O'Malley, cheeks ballooning. 'You can smoke, any of you, if you like.'

A gathering of non-smokers. A flashbulb flared. The room was one of the Kilkelly Castle Hotel's less criminally priced, being pokey, remote and damp : a single guest bedroom in the North Turret, locked and forgotten except during the peak season, without bath but with sticks of veneered furniture and the obligatory bosky papering on which dallied flouncing damsels and conquistadores with rapiers and ostrich plumes. In the wardrobe, stiff and twisted as driftwood, was Harvey.

'This wasn't his room, so someone lugged him up,' deduced O'Malley.

'I'll have a word with Sergeant Byrne,' muttered Mulligan, troubled. He had ordered Byrne to acquire a key, he believed. But then what? Had the key been acquired? The Inspector's memory was blank. Somewhere in the chain of command a fault had occurred. Someone, and not solely the Sergeant, had blundered.

Apart from the driftwood, in the turret room were Henry, Superintendent O'Malley, Inspector Mulligan, two junior gardai dedicated to tape-measures and fingerprint powder, Ramsey Gore and Dr Langer, who had brought, expendably, his black bag. A chambermaid with pass-key, foraging in readiness for an inventory, had found Harvey. Now she was tea-drinking at home, excused further duties for the day.

'Cause of death,' O'Malley said, 'bullet holes, but, how many?'

'Does it matter?' Dr Langer said.

'I can see four from here,' said O'Malley.

'He's dead is all I can say at the moment. By gunfire, presumably. Possibly three or four weeks ago. Further than that your forensics will have to fill you in.' Dr Langer's paunch billowed like a spinnaker. He wore an Aran jersey bought in the hotel shop, topaz slacks and waterproof golfing boots. 'I'm just a country doctor on vacation.'

'Most grateful, Doctor, most grateful.'

'How about your head, Mr Butt? Like me to take a look?'

Henry, half in, half out of the window, agreed he would like that. He sat on the window-sill while the country doctor unwound the old dressing, wound on a new.

He had missed his flight. Inspector Mulligan had can-celled the reservation and booked another for the next day. Meanwhile, Bodyguard Griffin would remain with him, wherever. In spite of the open window the air was fetid. Henry summoned his nerve and said to Dr Langer:

'Feet? That's to say, foot. It's Miss Kennedy.'

'Yes?' Dr Langer said.

'I'm terribly sorry, what with my head, and now, er, Mr Harvey. But Miss Kennedy, I'm told there's a doctor,

Dr Riley, only he's in Cork.' Henry turned away and gazed once more over parkland. 'I wouldn't even mention it but it looks like your golf is finished.'

Dr Langer and Henry stared together through the window. A suede-and-cashmere threesome had emerged from trees and were advancing on the eighteenth green.

'I was five down anyway,' Dr Langer said. 'She's at— where is it?'

'Carrigann. It's only twenty minutes in a car. You might remember her, she was a guest here, she's had this accident.'

'I'd heard. So let's start. Your car or mine?'

'Would that be all right?' Henry asked the Superintendent. 'This is Harvey, I can vouch for it. P. Harvey. I don't know what the P was for.'

'Pest,' said Gore.

'*De mortuis*,' said Inspector Mulligan.

Before Henry, doctor and bodyguard left, Superintendent O'Malley muttered in a corner with the bodyguard.

After they had left, he said to the Inspector:

'Curse that flight. Is there nothing sooner than tomorrow?'

'Nothing direct.'

'Get him something indirect. Route him through Astrakhan. I don't like him wandering about. Could we not lock him up till his plane leaves? Suspicion of malicious wounding of Miss Kennedy?'

'Griffin's solid enough. He should be all right.'

'Like in Carrigann with the guns blazing. Guns give me an urge to resign, John. D'you know I've not held a gun in twenty-five years, not since the army? What d'you make of the doctor?'

Inspector Mulligan, holding his breath, closed the wardrobe doors. The junior gardai were measuring carpeting and writing memoranda.

'Perhaps, Mr Gore, we could see you below, in a while,' the Inspector said.

'I want that thing away down the fire-escape,' the manager said.

'Won't be long, we're just finishing up.'

'What about this room? You realize labour costs, redecorating, all of that?'

'A burst of your air-freshener and she'll be fit for a potentate,' said the Inspector.

'Dr Langer's bill,' Gore said, 'is not the hotel's responsibility. I never asked for him.'

'We'll settle with Dr Langer.'

'And the telephoning? I've not noticed you keeping accounts.'

'All being recorded,' said the Inspector.

'Too many liberties, it's all very well.' Hands in blazer pockets, thumbs out, Gore groped in his mind for further liberties, but failed. 'Just don't carry that thing through my hotel, that's all.'

He strutted from the room.

Inspector Mulligan said, 'I don't know, I'd thought the doctor was just a doctor.'

The tape-measure tautened against his turn-up. He stepped over it and took up the window position vacated by Henry. ''Tis possible I'm not by nature suspicious. I'd say the doctor was clean. What d'ye make of the manager?'

'Old Balance-Sheet?' O'Malley said.

'Just a manager?'

'What're you driving at?'

'None of the guests have been here over the whole period during which McGrew vanished, Harvey was shot, and now Butt is bludgeoned. Right? Your man Langer's been here only ten days. But Gore covers the whole period.'

'So do the rest of the staff.'

'The rest of the staff are from hereabouts, more or less. Culchies out of your back farms. There's one or two like the cook might be handy with a blackthorn when the drink is on 'em, but as for guns.' The Inspector traced a finger through dust on the window-ledge. 'They'd have no more notion, with respect, than yourself.'

'A bit sweeping, wouldn't y' say?'

'I'd say we were after something more sophisticated.'

'Gore's as sophisticated as a herring.'

'He's got a record.'

'Fraud?'

'You knew?' Mulligan sounded disappointed.

'As treasurer of the Royal and Ancient Piddlesea Yacht Club, Major Gore, late of one of your dimmer British regiments, ransacked the petty cash.'

'Near enough. Only the petty cash was a quarter million from London Airport. Not that Gore's cut would have been any great shakes. He was a receptionist at that Skypilot Hotel where three of the gang holed up. Probably hadn't a notion what was going on. He got eighteen months.'

'When did he come out?'

'Seven years ago.'

'When did he buy this place?'

'Seven years ago.'

'Cash?'

'Cash. The money wasn't recovered.'

'That ties in,' said a voice. The startled expression of a junior garda appeared round the corner of the wardrobe. His shoulders were festooned with tape measure like a gentleman's outfitter.

'Haven't you finished yet?' Mulligan said.

The apparition withdrew.

'But at least he's a city boy, your convict,' O'Malley said.

'London,' Mulligan said.

'One of the Kensington Gores?'

'Pardon?'

'Granted. And at present he'll be your front-runner.'

'I'm not saying I buy him. But I don't think I buy your Yankee doctor.'

'You sound like the Daisy Market. Who else don't you buy?'

'The doctor's pals. Two are lawyers, the other makes laminated tiles or something. But they're good golfers, all of 'em. They're devils for it.'

'I don't follow your logic but likely the psychology's sound. What about the Kennedy woman, what's she up to?'

'She'll not be up to anything now her ankle is violated.'

'Y' know, John, we're tackling this from the wrong end.' Hand clamped on hat, Superintendent O'Malley edged the Inspector aside and leaned out of the window.

'The question's why, not who. Find out why and we'll get who.'

'Find out who,' the Inspector said, 'and we needn't fuss about why.'

'Has the pond been dragged?'

'Twice.'

'Better do it again.' The Superintendent re-entered the room. 'First, I want the hotel searched. Don't tell me you've already done it. This place has more empty rooms than a museum. Use your nose. Every closet and broom cupboard and laundry shaft. Next thing we know the tourists will be tramping in and some fancy filum star in her négligee will be snuggling into bed and finding McGrew has beaten her to it.'

'And in no state to give her satisfaction.'

'Didn't McGrew go astray two weeks before Harvey?'

'First of March. Harvey was the day before St Patrick's Day.'

'So if McGrew's still here he'll likely be a bit fresh. Go on the assumption he's somewhere about, and find him. I'm off to Carrigann.'

'Looking for McGrew?'

'Just looking,' O'Malley said. 'If we come up with any real answers, John, it'll be at Carrigann. This place is an irrelevance.'

'I'd not call that corpse an irrelevance.'

The Inspector accompanied his chief out of the room, along the corridor, past locked rooms. Being a recondite turret of the hotel, penetrated only at the height of the season, the corridor walls were not pastoral, or Regency, or William Morris flock, but yellow paint.

'What,' said O'Malley, 'have our three victims in common? I suppose 'tis two-and-a-half since Mr Butt's still breathing. I hope.'

'Griffin's a solid lad.'

'You said that. Listen. McGrew, Harvey, Butt. They're miners, isn't that it? So the answer to why is where they're mining. The why is the where, if you follow. In a cavern, in a canyon, excavating in Carrigann. You know the trouble, John?'

The pair halted at the head of stairs leading down. Mulligan rested a moody hand on the yellow banister post, awaiting the trouble. He wanted neither the trouble nor to return to the sorting out of stiff Harvey.

O'Malley said, 'If Butt stays, someone will try another crack at him, wouldn't y' say? But once he's gone, how do we find out what's going on under the ground?'

'He's not the only miner.'

'He's the only Canuck miner, John, and at this rate I'll lay odds he's the last. Then what? What'll your Inspector's pay be worth if next thing they're placing bullets in your darlin' Mick miners?'

CHAPTER X

In contrast to Ramsey Gore's echoing fortress, the Carrigann Park Hotel teemed.

The cousins Cooney and Flynn had struck gold, or would have done so had they been more current with prices and such fripperies as service charges and presentation of bills. Not only was each of the seven guest rooms taken, and clearly would continue to be taken for as long as Ivernia shares held, but all space behind doors, available and unavailable, had been converted. To open a random door was to enter a former pantry or storage room which, while presenting the piled evidence of its earlier function (paint pots, tea chests, old magazines, wellington boots, a bag of pig-feed), now also housed a hammock or inflated air-bed, and the suitcase of an immigrant. Conversion was a word much on the lips of the cousins. They had as yet had little time in which to start converting, but they had pencilled rough sketches on envelopes and discussed the advisability of damp-courses and the geography of room-partitioning with a frequenter of Egan's who claimed experience of the building trade in England. The house was old but structurally sound, they believed. They had a three-year plan, a five-year plan, a six-year plan (by which stage they would be in the swimming-pool and chauffeured tours category), and a provisional, slightly misty ten-year plan (heliport, covered shopping area, visiting heads of state).

More immediately, priorities were eradication of seepage, reinforcement of the uncertain staircase up to the third floor, and implementation (as Cooney liked to call it) of the check-list of demands thrust at them by officialdom. Prominent on the check-list of demands were additional toilets, a battery of regulations pertaining to fire hazard, and disposal for sanitary reasons of the seventeen greyhounds in the basement labyrinth. Quotations for three new toilets, two with bathroom suites, were being solicited, but these matters took a day or two, Cooney was able to tell an inspector who one wild March morning had arrived in person. Flynn, plucking

the jackeen's sleeve, had pointed in pride to a glittering
fire-extinguisher mounted and still plastic-wrapped in
the front hall, and on the first-floor landing to a bucket
of soil and a coil of rope; all of which, Cooney had
explained, were merely a beginning. As to the dogs,
negotiations for sale were proceeding but Rome hadn't
been built in a day. (Negotiations were not proceeding,
they had not started, though the cousins had agreed
between themselves to sell or give away the four greyhounds which were no longer nimble enough to get
round a track and were proving, to boot, bad breeders.
All seventeen they had shifted only the previous week
into the shed at the southern end of the walled garden,
where their yelping due to starvation passed unheard.
The cousins had good intentions for feeding and exercis-
ing the animals but what with one thing and another,
their welfare had been neglected.)

Perambulating livestock cropped in the grounds, inhibiting the savagery in its urge to take over, and in-
doors a swift splash with a paintbrush settled the nonsense of the flakier patches of brown. But sensibly the
proprietors of Carrigann Park had opted to defer gardening, painting, decorating and fancywork until more
basic needs had been met, such as instalment of central
heating. And with summer coming on they had decided
to postpone central heating and concentrate on the
holed roof over the stables, now renamed by Cooney the
West Annex, and referred to as such whenever he, or
Flynn, remembered.

Staff, they were finding, were a problem, particularly
on days when there were none, but the Devlin sisters
could normally be relied on for kitchen work, and most

mornings Mrs O'Finneran came in to arrange flowers.
Mrs O'Finneran's mother, known to guests as the White
Cyclone, might be sighted on Wednesday afternoons as
she gusted through passages and up stairways embrac-
ing cloths, mops, brooms, basins, Brasso, Brillo, Windo-
lene, Ajax, Harpic and O-Cedar, skirts swishing, soapy
water squirting, a dust-devouring maelstrom, jousting
with cobwebs, lancing at mice, and leaving in her wake
forgotten mounds of floor-sweepings and smells of wax
polish and ammonia. The proprietors were frequently
surprised to note how their establishment thrived without such standard fixtures as porters, receptionists, wait-
resses, boot-blacks and hotel detectives. In lieu there
was ample parking space, rustic views, birdsong and a
merry pioneering air of makeshift. A guest with a com-
plaint might be soothed with words and a drink, or if
these failed he could seek a roof elsewhere, and good
luck, the nearest alternative being the Kilkelly Castle.
There were no locks at Carigann Park, no keys, and
no traveller was turned away. Everyone could be
squeezed in somewhere. The arrival of Kate had brought
the guest complement up to twenty-seven.

When Kate's taxi, a charred saloon with yellow mudguards driven by Proprietor Billy Dunne, had foundered
thirteen miles out of Kilkelly, Kate had faced a choice
of either walking back to Kilkelly or two miles sideways
to Carrigann, where she could seek another taxi, which
did not exist, or a room, which, at Carrigann Park, did.
This particular room, puny and airless, had served
mixed purposes over the years, and until Kate's arrival
had been the sleeping quarters of Flynn and Cooney.
Impedimenta of previous occupants had assembled like

talismen in a pharaoh's tomb: piano, saddle, music-stand, birdcage, ping-pong table propped in halves against a wall, painter's palette, a pile of decomposing ledgers, heaped books, clothing, saucers. On the marble mantelpiece over the fireplace stood religious curios, a Madonna-shaped bottle of holy water from Lourdes, a half-eaten chocolate bar. Above the camp-bed a framed oleograph in primary colours of the Sacred Heart. On the camp-bed, in tweeds, shoeless and unstockinged, lay Kate.

'This might sting just for a second,' Dr Langer said, dabbing antiseptic.

'It's all right,' Henry assured her, a laugh in his voice. For Kate's sake he wanted cheeriness to break through. Good humour was infectious. She was sour now but later she would understand. 'You should see it, it's nothing.'

'Go away,' Kate said.

'No, believe me, you can take my word, it's clean, a clean wound.'

'What do you—ow!' Kate winced. Antiseptic overlayed the room's earlier, unidentifiable smells. 'What do you know about it?'

Henry, discouraged, fell silent. Bodyguard Griffin, by removing his cap, holding it against his chest, and wheeling it in spasms between fists as big as pumpkins, projected into the room an air of last rites, imminent decease. Such nearness to a grown, naked-footed woman made him uneasy, as it had made Garda Feeney uneasy. Griffin, Henry and the dismembered ping-pong table occupied between them most of the room space. Flynn stood wedged by Cooney against the wall with one boot

among saucers. Griffin whispered to Henry: 'I'm t'inkin'
we'd best wait outside.'

No one moved. Exhilarated, open-mouthed, Cooney
and Flynn watched the medical procedure. They had
flinched at the tetanus shot, tensed at the cleansing of
the wound, and now watched the bandaging with the
concentration of medical students about to sit for a
crucial bandaging examination. Dr Langer bandaged
dexterously and, to Cooney's eye, extravagantly.

'That's a deal of bandage!' Cooney said.

"Tis crêpe,' Flynn said.

'I know 'tis crêpe,' said Cooney. 'Listen, d'ye think
we have need of a first-aid box?'

'Whatever for?'

'Here, in the hotel. For the accidents.'

'What accidents?'

'Here's an accident for a start,' Cooney said, pointing
at Kate. 'I'm not sayin' there'll be accidents. All I'm
sayin' is, prevention is the best cure.'

'We're not a hospital, we'll not be doin' the trans-
plants,' Flynn said.

'Where is the nearest hospital?' Dr Langer asked. He
pinned the bandage. Kate's foot and leg were bandaged
from toes to upper calf. 'I'd like you to have it X-rayed,
Kate. Just to be safe.'

'Mallow,' Garda Griffin said. 'That'll be the nearest.'

'You said there was no bone damage,' Henry said.

'It's as well to have the X-ray.' Dr Langer looked
about for a bin into which to drop a pad of bloody lint.
Seeing none he tossed the pad into the grate. 'If the bone
has been touched, it's all a little different.'

'We'll not be doin' any kiss o' life,' Flynn told his

cousin. 'I'll not mind the first-aid box but we're not fiddlin' with kiss o' life or any o' that massage stuff.'

'My ankle,' Kate sobbed.

'Heel,' said Henry, 'it's the heel, not the ankle. What was that word, Doctor?'

'Calcaneum?'

'Calcaneum. It's just a grazed calcaneum. If it'd been the ankle you'd have had to have plaster. You're all right.'

'I can't walk!'

'You'll have to wear a slipper,' Dr Langer said, and clipped shut his black bag. 'You should be able to manage with a slipper. Do you have a roomy one?'

'No.'

'I have!' Henry's liberality was unrestrained. 'Roomy and soft!'

'Not,' Dr Langer started to say, 'too soft at the heel—'

'No, no, it's firm there, at the heel.' Not, heaven knew, that he was responsible for Miss Kennedy's mishap, but Henry's conscience, his overdeveloped sense of responsibility, would be assuaged by a slipper. Partially, at least. Treading on the birdcage, Henry stepped back and drew Cooney aside, towards the sections of propped ping-pong table. He assumed a conspiratorial smile and an undertone. 'I suppose, ha-ha, you haven't a spare room for tonight?'

'Gob, we have,' Cooney said.

'You have?'

'I'll fix you up. You'll not mind if 'tis a wee bit obstructed? You didn't book in advance, y' see.'

'That's okay, great, I go back to Canada tomorrow, my bags are outside. The problem is, would there be space, do you think, for the guard? Somewhere?'

'Him?'

'It's complicated but, well, if I stay, he has to stay.
Can you fit him in?'

''Tis Jimmy Griffin's boy, is it not? Wait a tick.'

Cooney leaned to the left and consulted with Flynn.
Dr Langer had cleared a space on the mantelpiece and
was writing a note among bric-a-brac. Cooney leaned
to the right.

''Twill be all right for one night but tomorrow we've
this coach party, don't y' see. A convention. A long-
stand booking.' Cooney did not look Henry in the eyes
but off-centre, in the direction of the ear-lobes. 'A
garda about the place, it'd look queer, you understand
that?'

'Understand that,' Flynn said.

'I'll call this Mallow hospital and warn them you're
coming,' Dr Langer told Henry, handing him whatever
he had been writing, 'and if you give them this, it'll
put them in the picture.' To Kate he said, 'Well, Kate.
I'll look in tomorrow.'

Flynn led the doctor away to telephone.

Henry, bodyguard at his elbow, collected his suitcases from the garda car, was hospitably relieved of
them, and followed Cooney back into the house, up
the stairs, and through the empty dining-room. The trio
halted at the far end of the dining-room, in the yawning
convexity of a bay window looking out over the drive
and fields at the front of Carrigann Park. Henry re-
garded the view. The horizon was mauve mountains.

'Breathtaking,' he said. 'Are they the Galtee?'

Cooney put down the suitcases, reached up, and

jerked a sacking curtain across the alcove.

'I'll seek out a pair of mattresses,' he said. 'We've a heap of fine mattresses if I can lay my hands on them. Interior-sprung.' He jerked the curtains back, then across again, then back, as though signalling. 'Your garda can be right in the room with you, y' see. We don't mind.'

'You mean, this is it?'

'Or if you favour privacy, you can have the curtain between you.' The curtain flourished back across the alcove, demonstrating privacy.

Henry emitted a sigh that was partly a moan. He told himself to stay calm. 'Except that he'll be in the dining-room.'

'I'd say on the circumference of it. And there's little enough eating after nine.'

Bodyguard Griffin stood silently, unwavering.

Of the twenty or thirty points Henry wished to raise he selected, simply, 'It's only one night.'

'And when you get home,' Cooney breathed, leaning close, 'if you could just pass the word round. You'll be a man with connections. Many of our clientele are by personal recommendation.'

Henry believed that under the bright new bandage his head was starting to trouble him again. He crouched by a suitcase, unlocked it, and began rooting for a roomy slipper.

CHAPTER XI

Roomy as a bath, the slipper adhered to Kate's foot only because of the stuffing of newspapers and socks plus the additional sock in merry tartan which had been drawn over the whole and up to her knee. The socks as well as the slipper were Henry's, and the stuffed, crumpled newspapers inside the slipper were the *Cork Examiner*. Tartan-footed Kate gripped a walking-stick. Huddled in a corner of the travelling garda car's back seat, as far away as possible from the massive myopic pink obsolete plesiosaurus in the opposite corner, she looked like a gouty Scotsman being chauffeured to a cure in the Trossachs.

Chauffeur Griffin, Mallow-bound, glanced in the rear-view mirror and said, after hesitation, "'Tis a grand evenin' then.'

What he had wanted to say was, 'Holy Mother, that gouger's still followin'!'

Henry said, 'How much farther?'

'Another fifteen minutes should do it, sor,' the body-guard said, and accelerated along the country road.

Round the next bend Griffin braked, dropping the garda car's speed from sixty to thirty. He looked in the mirror and saw the green sports car swarm round the curve, then slow, keeping its distance.

The policeman accelerated again. His inexperienced wits churned. If the green car was after mischief the two-way radio would be no use here in the thick of nowhere, except for filling the lady and gentleman with anxiousness. And what if he were mistaken? What if the green car were a bookie late for the greyhound racing but terrified to overtake the gardai?

Griffin accelerated harder. The needle on the speedometer crawled to seventy.

'Hold tight, sor and miss!' he called as a new bend rushed towards the car.

He rounded the bend at seventy-two, then braked. Kate and Henry lurched forward from their corners.

'Hell!' exclaimed Henry from the floor.

'My ankle!'

'A pig, I was avoidin' a pig,' Griffin cried, eyes on the mirror. 'Did yez not see her dive for safety?'

The green car swung on screaming tyres round the curve, past the stationary garda car, and on into the distance.

'And the drunken drivers,' elaborated Griffin, writing in his notebook the green car's registration. 'Did yez see that one? We'll give 'im a minute for clearance. Then I'll find a phone-box.'

'My ankle!'

'Is it damaged?' Henry had regained the seat. Solicitous, he bent forward.

'I don't think so. I had it lifted up. Like this.'

'Good. Yes. That would have protected it.'

'It feels the same but the sudden movement might have stirred it up.'

Kate and Henry peered closely at the tartan. They held their breath, waiting for a sign. The car started moving forward.

'It's not the ankle, you know, it's the heel,' Henry

explained. 'The calcaneum.'

'All right, the calcaneum.'

Suddenly irritable, realizing the proximity of the pink plesiosaurus, and remembering her hostility to him, Kate moved back into her corner.

'That was a pretty dangerous stunt,' Henry told the bodyguard, retiring into his own corner, irritable because Kate was irritable. If she were not prepared to see reason, to meet him half-way, well, hell, he might let her stew. He said to Griffin, 'You ought to watch your driving.'

'I will, sor,' Griffin said, shifting the gear into fourth. The road ahead was deserted. 'I'd like to lay me hands on them drunken acrobats.'

'You can do that at the Kilkelly Castle, they're staying there,' Kate said.

'What?'

'How—?'

'Yez saw—?'

'You mean you—?'

'Anyone with eyes could have seen them,' Kate said, and looked away through the window, disdainful.

'And yez say,' Griffin said, 'they're at the Kilkelly Castle?'

'They are. Or were. I'm not to know if they're there still.'

'Two of 'em, is it?'

'It is.'

'And do yez know their names?'

'I do not.'

'Local?'

'Foreigners, I'm sure.'

'Bleddy foreigners,' Griffin muttered, addressing the windshield.

Cerebrating deeply, the bodyguard dropped the gear into third and drove through a nameless village smaller than Carrigann and without zinc and lead enthusiasms to ripple its calm. Sunk in the skin between the bodyguard's eyes were frown lines like climbing bars in a gymnasium. The eyes shifted from left to right, watching for the green sports car. Where the village merged again into country stood a phone-box. Griffin parked beside it.

'I must request yez to remain where yez are. I'll only be a tick.'

Watching the village with one eye, his charges in the garda car with the other, Griffin phoned Inspector Mulligan at the Kilkelly Castle Hotel. Inspector Mulligan was not available, but Sergeant Byrne was, still smarting from the Inspector's shafts over that incomprehensible matter of keys and some gouger's body in the North Turret of Kilkelly Castle. The sergeant took down the green car's number, then entered upon careful, complex instructions.

'I will, Sarge, yes, right so, Sarge, count on me, Sarge,' agreed Bodyguard Griffin into the phone, eyeing the moribund street. When a wide-shouldered character carrying a spare car tyre approached along the pavement, Griffin leaned against the kiosk door, easing it open. He slid his boot into the opening, ready to leap, to interpose official bone and muscle between his charges and the character. The character, shambling past, gawped through the glass at the garda. In the back of the garda car the man and woman sat with space enough between them for a string orchestra.

'Thank yez for yez patience,' the bodyguard told the man and woman, driving off.

The climbing bars returned as he repeated to himself the sergeant's interminable instructions. Take away the gas and blather and these instructions, so far as Garda Griffin could make out, added up to the following: If anything happens to either of those two, you'll be for it, so watch it.

Griffin watched the road unwind ahead, the side roads, the road behind. He overtook an ancient Rolls-Royce with straw on its back bumper; a lesser, shinier vehicle propelled sluggishly by one of a party of nuns; a child cyclist; an infant pedestrian; and a vivid tourist caravan, horse-drawn, and steered by an English couple steeped in nostalgia for the streets of Hemel Hempstead. He was passed by sparse, assorted cars coming from the opposite direction. But no green sports cars.

'How is it now?' Henry asked Kate.

'How is what?'

Never mind then, if that's how you're going to be, Henry decided; and turning an upholstered fleecy scapula in her direction he stared out on the bungaloid fringes of Mallow.

Kate thought: Now I've been too rude. He's trying, poor man. I don't care. He's too big. It's all his fault.

Henry took out his pocketbook and found the note given him by Dr Langer. The bodyguard found the hospital. Twenty minutes after entering the hospital the two men and Kate returned to the garda car. Henry kept repeating, 'Incredible, just incredible.' Never had he encountered such amiable efficiency. In around six minutes the X-ray had been accomplished, the bone visibly shown to be unscathed, and the radiologist's written confirmation promised for the morning. Most of the time had been occupied in undressing and dressing Kate's foot. 'Amazing,' Henry murmured as his bodyguard slid the car through traffic lights and across a bridge over the Blackwater.

'You'd think we were in the jungle the way you go on,' Kate said. 'What's that jungle place called?'

'The Everglades?'

'Where?'

'I'm not exactly sure what you mean.'

'Where that man was. The organist.'

'Schweitzer? Lambaréné?'

'That's it. We're not prehistoric, you know.'

'No, no. I wasn't suggesting you were. On the contrary—'

'Does anyone mind if we have a sausage roll or something?' Kate inquired. 'I've had nothing since breakfast. Can we not halt for chips?'

Cheered by the hospital experience, as pleased with herself as if she had personally assisted W. K. Röntgen in discovering X-rays, Kate realized she was hungry. Looking at his watch, Henry saw that the time was only five-thirty. He had arrived in Ireland little more than twenty-four hours ago. Garda Griffin turned the wheel and headed back into town.

Kate made the selection, and on the outside Evangeline's Restaurant wore a confident air. Inside, it was empty. The tables were miniature and close together, and round the tops of ketchup bottles clung congealed red collars. Kate chose a table by the lace-curtained window. Murmuring about proprieties, responsibilities, being in uniform, on duty, and how Sor and Miss should feel fully free to converse between themselves, Garda Griffin lowered himself on to a creaking chair at a table by the door and ordered from the girl-child who arrived in the role of waitress ('That's Little Evangeline,' Kate whispered, sunny at the prospect of food), sausages, beans, double chips, four rounds of bread and butter, and a glass of water.

'I think I might wait,' Henry told Kate, examining the menu, 'until we get back to the hotel.'

'You mean the Carrigann Park Hotel?'

'Well, yes.'

'Ha!'

'I expect you're right. What do you suggest then?'

'I'm having steak.' To Little Evangeline, Kate said, 'Quite rare, please, and salad.'

'I'll have the same,' Henry said. 'Do you have a wine list?'

'Soft drinks or tea,' said Little Evangeline.

Henry sniffed snuff up his nostrils. Kate ducked, but with handkerchief clamped to nose Henry swivelled on his chair and trumpeted in the direction of Garda Griffin.

He sniffed again in the garda car, bounding back towards Carrigann, and sneezed out of the window.

'God save us!' Kate cried.

'Sorry.' Henry swallowed, gasped. 'It clears the head.'

'It near blows yours off. Isn't it a drug, that stuff, like tobacco?'

'It is tobacco—pulverized tobacco.'

'Is that so? Are you an addict?'

'I don't know, I only started last month.' Henry lifted his glasses and swabbed his eyes. 'There was a time it was thought medicinal, two hundred years ago. Lots of women took it. Would you like a pinch?'

'A pinch?'

'The snuff.'

'I would not.' Kate started to laugh. 'Thanks all the same.'

They passed through the village smaller than Carrigann. A troop of male residents had materialized on the pavement outside a pub and were leaning against its wall, discussing. Into open country, accelerating, fled the garda car, its heavyweight driver alert for signs of mischief, watchful for a green sports car, but failing to sight it, though the car was there, clinging, holding back, out of view, a quarter of a mile, sometimes half a mile behind.

'Perhaps,' Kate said, simultaneously thrilled and anxious as she took this step into the unknown, 'the tiniest speck, just to try.'

'Good. Here, help yourself.' Henry removed the lid of his snuff tin. 'Go steady the first time.'

Kate, paper tissue poised, went so very steady, pinching such a timorous speck, that nothing, other than a merest tickle, occurred. Suppressing giggles, she dug deeper into the brown dust with a finger nail, sniffed, and sneezed triumphantly.

'I don't know as I'd, ah, want to make a, ooh, habit of it,' she panted, leaning back, dabbing her eyes.

'You can get different flavours,' Henry said. 'This one's mentholated.'

After a moment, Kate said, 'I'm sorry you didn't get your wine.'

'That's all right. We might be able to find some in

Carrigann, if you'd like that, if you'd care to join me.'
Before she could accept or reject, Henry prattled on,
'I was rather wanting to see part of the site first, if
there's time. Er, Constable—Officer?' Henry touched
the bodyguard on the shoulder. 'What time does it get
dark?'

About another hour or so, Garda Griffin thought, she
should start closin' in, sor.

'I suppose you wouldn't know where that Ivernia drill
was broken exactly? There was a drill smashed up about
five weeks ago. End of February, I think.'

'Twould be the end of February precisely, or early
March, Garda Griffin agreed. Wasn't himself on the
very spot in the course of his duties, assisting Inspector
Mulligan only the morning after, sor?

'That'll be fine, if you could take me, and Miss Kennedy—if you'd care to come, Kate—just for a look,
I'd quite like just to look, while I'm here.'

Six hundred yards behind, the Common Market clerks
in their green sports car took a bend and saw ahead,
pinbox-sized on a rare stretch of straight road, the black
garda car. The sports car's driver slowed. His colleague,
motionless by his side, watched the distant car without
comment.

They had twice botched this job and they were pro-
fessionals, or supposed to be. If they were to stay in
the game there could be no question of fumbling a third
time.

CHAPTER XII

Hairy Zeus, controlling the weather from his throne atop a mountain peak in Greece, studied the barometer on his lap. His daughter Artemis, set for a day's hunting, leaned over his shoulder and tapped the barometer with her riding-crop. She wore a riding-hat and jodhpurs. Apollo, her twin-brother, god of songs, doctors and prophecy, wore nothing. He sat on a rock bandaging his foot and looking less beautiful than the myths had led one to believe. His belly, in fact, more Dionysiac than Apollonian, was moon-shaped, and the facial features were those of Dr Langer. Sharing his rock, pulling four-by-two through the barrel of an anachronistic carbine (It's not true, none of it's true, Superintendent O'Malley dreamed, stirred into semi-consciousness) sat war-goddess Athena in steel helmet.

In winged helmet, trudging up Olympus towards this domestic scene, came a postman carrying a parcel.

'Hermes,' O'Malley said, awaking with relief from his cat-nap.

Hermes: another son of Zeus, inventor of the lyre, god of commerce, messenger of the gods. Wasn't that it? The winged helmet had been the giveaway. Or should it have been winged sandals? Or winged both? God, there'd been a time, in boyhood, in his mythology days, when he'd not have been in doubt about a detail like that. He'd have to look it up some time. If he remembered.

He looked instead at his watch. John Mulligan would be another ten minutes, quite possibly. There was time for a quick glass.

Was there anything he should be usefully doing instead? In the fug of the Ford Zodiac parked in Carrigann's main street, O'Malley tilted back his trampled, gravy-brown hat and flicked open a notebook. The afternoon, since the finding of Harvey, had brought two developments. Three, if the tiresome failure to turn up McGrew could be counted as a development. Almost certainly McGrew was not in the Kilkelly Castle Hotel, which in its way was a development. What had they done with the feller? Dissolved him in acid? Buried him deep with the zinc and lead?

One. Failure to turn up McGrew.

Two. Success in tracing McGrew's gun. Not, that was to say, McGrew's gun, or probably not, but the gun found in the herbaceous border below McGrew's hotel room. A plant. (A plant in the herbaceous border, mused fanciful O'Malley, mind starting to wander, gazing through the window at the jostling street. He resolved to be firm with himself, to apply his thoughts.) Someone had planted the gun because McGrew, so far as anyone knew, had no cause to possess a gun, and killers capable of making a victim disappear so comprehensively did not drop their firearms in herbaceous borders, or anywhere else. So the gun was a red herring, bought second-hand in a Cork gunshop on February 28 by a Mr Merlin of no distinguishing features so far as the gunsmith could recall, not one, and a non-existent Cork address.

Three. (O'Malley watched urchins in a potato-crate

chariot rumble down the middle of the street. One urchin pushed, the weediest of the group, while the others berated him for not pushing more effectively.) Failure to locate a green sports car (JZA 622), last seen by Garda Griffin overtaking him and vanishing at a steady lick in the direction of Mallow. Whether this would be the same green sports car from which Miss Kennedy had been shot in the second attempt on Mr Butt's life, was uncertain. There was doubt whether the car carrying the gunmen in Carrigann had been a green sports car. Mr Butt had said it was green but he had been in a bandaged and unsettled state, and another witness, a farmer's wife of established unreliability, had thought the car was a black Volkswagen ('One o' dem Jerry jobs wid de engine back to front, y' know?'). Further doubt existed about the occupants of JZA 622, but as Miss Kennedy had believed she had seen these two at the Kilkelly Castle, and as the Messrs Nagel and Gallone, the only male pair staying at that hotel, had checked out that morning, she might well be right. Picking them up, and JZA 622, ought to be only a matter of time.

Time, on the other hand, was running out. If the green sports car got past Garda Griffin, and to Mr Butt, before Mr Butt boarded his plane around this same time tomorrow, there'd likely be a nasty mess. Butt's bodyguard, the Superintendent decided, starting to worry, would have to be doubled. Trebled. Ideally the man should be locked up. Only that would mean prickly questions in high places.

And tomorrow (the piled potato-crate returned down the street, grinding like a tank), before the plane, he'd take Butt and a bodyguard of two dozen for a closer scout round the boreholes. It was the why, dammit, not the who.

'Would you get on to control,' O'Malley told his sergeant driver, 'and tell them to ask Griffin and Mr Butt to please get back to their hotel right away. Whatever it's called. I'll see them there.'

The Superintendent stepped out into the dusk. All afternoon the rain had held off. Now fat drops were starting to fall. He settled his hat rigidly on his head. 'If Inspector Mulligan arrives, I'll be back in five minutes.'

The sergeant was speaking into the two-way radio, and Superintendent O'Malley pushing open the door into Egan's, at the moment when Garda Griffin switched on the windscreen wipers. He swung the wheel and turned off the Carrigann-Shanballymore road. They had called briefly at the Carrigann Park Hotel for Henry, bodyguard by his side, to collect a canvas satchel from his suitcase. In his private alcove behind the sacking curtain, Henry had been vaguely surprised to find his cases undisturbed. On the stairs they had passed Flynn carrying a cabbage in each hand. 'The choux must go on,' Henry had said brightly, and Flynn had grinned without comprehension, showing mole-grey stubs of teeth.

In the garda car, wipers swishing, the bodyguard said, 'First lane past that cottage, that's Mrs O'Hare's, then up the boreen and we're there, sor.'

'Good,' said Henry. 'It's not getting any lighter.'

'It's getting a deal wetter,' Kate said. 'Do we have to walk about in a field?'

'Isn't it the rain that gives Irish girls such beautiful complexions?' Henry said, and immediately felt self-conscious. 'I'm sure it's stopping.'

The bodyguard parked on the brow of a grassy track and switched off the wipers. All round were fields. Rain pattered lightly on the roof.

'There, sor.' Garda Griffin pointed. 'Left of the shed, in a line with the tree. Yez can see where the earth was t'rown up.'

'I see it.'

'They've took away the drillin' apparatus.'

Signs of the field having known life other than sheep and cows were the half-begun borehole fifty yards distant, criss-crossing tracks of weighty vehicles which had churned grass into mud, and a workman's mobile hut which no one had found enthusiasm enough to remove.

'I'll wait here,' Kate said. 'I'd be up to my knees in that bog.'

'Don't worry about the sock. It'll wash.'

'Go on so. Call me if there's gold.'

Henry and his bodyguard trod through thin rain across the field.

'On a fine day yez can see the Galtee clear as yez fist,' the bodyguard said.

The abandoned borehole was a dozen square yards of trodden grass, earth and stones converging upon the hole itself, a muddy black aperture where the drill had sunk. There were cigarette ends, the wrapping of a chocolate bar. Henry took from his satchel a flashlight and shone it down the hole. Heads almost touching, bandage and peaked garda cap, the two men stooped and looked.

'I looked before, sor. There's nothing.'

'I doubt they got as far as the corer. All they've had here's the chipper.'

'Is that the trut'?'

Henry straightened up, switched off the flashlight, scraped at earth with his shoe. Slowly he walked round the borehole, eyes on the ground. He picked up a stone, glanced at it, threw it away. He found another with a splintered edge which the drill had flung up from underground. He rubbed earth from the stone with his thumb, held it close to his glasses, then tossed it aside. Still searching the ground he started walking in a widening spiral away from the borehole.

'See, sor,' said Griffin, approaching with a chunk of rock. 'What about this?'

Henry squinted at the rock, grunted, shook his head. He continued his slow spiralling, leaving the bodyguard disconsolately eyeing the rock in his sprawling hands.

'Hullo-o-o-o-o!' hullooed Kate.

She was advancing through the bog like a war veteran back from the front line, hobbling on one good foot and a walking-stick, handbag dangling, the tartan foot swinging free before descending toe first to the grass in a tentative dabbing motion.

'Hullo there!' She waved her stick in greeting. 'What're you doing?'

'Prospecting!' Henry called back.

'Gold?'

'Not so far!'

The rain had ceased, or almost. Henry stood tapping at something in his hand with the wedge end of a hammer. He threw the something away and returned the hammer to the satchel slung on a strap across his shoulder.

'What was that?' Kate wanted to know, a little out of breath. She stood beside him, searching with her eyes the spot into which he had cast away the something.

'Rubbish.'

'Have you not found anything?'

'Nope.'

'What are you looking for?'

'I don't know.'

'No, tell me.'

'It's a fact. Probably nothing. I just wanted to see. Give me another five minutes.'

'But that's silly. How will you find anything if you don't know what you're looking for?'

'Exactly the point. I shan't know what I'm looking for until I find it.' Henry circled slowly on, away from her, kicking at an infrequent stone in the grass, stooping to stare through pebble-lenses, walking on. 'How's the foot?'

'All right, thanks. I'm afraid your sock's soggy.'

Henry made no reply, but after a moment murmured, 'Fine.'

He's not interested, he's just asking, Kate realized, surprised to find herself not annoyed but amused. Typical man, preoccupied, not listening, she thought. This one, the geologist, over there on his hands and knees, was like a child at the seaside, seeking shells. The uniformed one standing beside her with a dirty stone held between thumb and forefinger as though it were the Koh-i-noor was even more of a child.

'Miss, what about this?'

Kate leaned back as the Koh-i-noor was positioned beneath her nose. She glanced up at the policeman. He was watching her keenly, restraining his excitement.

'What about it?'

'Do yez not spy anything different?'

'Where?'

'Look.'

'I am looking. It's a stone.'

'What about the silver?'

'What silver?'

'There, see?'

'That?'

''Tis silver, isn't it? Like at the mines in Limerick?'

'It's a shellicky bookey.'

For a moment the garda's expression remained unchanged. Then the suppressed excitement dropped away. He started to scratch with his fingernail at the silvery streak across the stone. Kate was doubled forward with laughter.

'An old shellicky bookey! Silver, he says!'

Garda Griffin, examining his fingernail, began to laugh. He licked his fingertip and rubbed it over the silver.

'We've struck shellicky bookeys!' hooted Kate, rocking and laughing, the tip of her walking-stick digging deeper into the mud, drilling its own borehole. 'We've got a shellicky bookey mine!'

Griffin laughed in a low rumbling key, like a volcano issuing warning to all inhabitants in a twenty-mile radius. 'A shellicky bookey mine,' he boomed. 'I'll buy two shares!'

'Listen,' Kate gasped, 'd'you know the song?

'*Shellicky shellicky bookey,*' Kate sang.

'*Put out all your horns,*' Kate and bodyguard sang together, discordant in the gathering dark and wet.

They stumbled singing through the field to where Henry, on hands and knees, was again hammering at a chunk of rock.

'*All the ladies are coming to see-e-e-e you.*'

Henry looked up.

'He thought it was silver,' Kate told Henry, 'and it's a shellicky bookey.'

Henry blinked, ready to enter the fun.

'A snail,' Kate explained.

The mining engineer in the wet grass failed to comprehend. 'Look at this,' he said, holding out his hand.

Kate and the bodyguard looked down at the lump of rock in Henry's hand. Ashamed at his loss of control, but now recovered, Garda Griffin cleared his throat. He could think of nothing to say.

'Lead?' Kate suggested.

The mining engineer shook his head.

'Zinc,' hazarded Garda Griffin.

'Cinnabar,' Henry said.

Kate and Garda Griffin stared blankly at the rock.

CHAPTER XIII

Nagel and Gallone, swart Latin clerks from some rose-red city half as old as crime, parked the green sports car lower down the boreen and switched off its side-lights at the moment Kate took the rock in her hand.

She could not decide whether she had met the word before Henry uttered it, or not. The Cinnabar Kid? Quinquireme of Cinnabar from distant Ophir? 'Do sample the cinnabar, Irene, it's fresh-baked today.'

'Cinnabar,' Henry repeated, 'I'm certain of it. I've seen it mined in Mexico. And in California—we had a sample for analysis in graduate school, you separate the metal by applying heat in an air current, then you purify by vacuum distillation. This is it, it really is. See that edge, where the drill cut through? It's here, under us. Cinnabar.' Repetitious, circular, gabbling with hardly a breath, Henry came to an abrupt stop. Then added, 'The chief ore of mercury.'

'Mercury.'

'Right, yes, it's ridiculous, there's no record I know of cinnabar in Ireland, but you see it figures because cinnabar,' galloped Henry, 'is a sulphide like galena which is the chief ore of lead and you often get galena with blende which is the ore of zinc, like here, in lodes and disseminations, all round, and in a mineralized area like this you'll get this assemblage of minerals in a whole metallogenetic province.' He took a breath. 'It's a sulphide the same as magnetic pyrites which is nickel's ore. You see? The biggest nickel deposits are at Sudbury.'

'Mercury like in thermometers?' Kate said.

'Sudbury, Ontario.' Henry's voice had dropped a semitone. He sounded sheepish. He shifted his two hundred and fifteen pounds of avoirdupois from one foot to the other. 'That's where I was born, Sudbury.'

'Like in a barometer?' Garda Griffin said, accepting from Kate, for expert analysis, the rock that was cinnabar.

'Barometers, yes, let's just look some more,' Henry said, back again from Sudbury, excited, hauling from his satchel the flashlight. 'Someone's done some cleaning up but we might find more. Judging by that bit, the drill must have thrown up a fair amount. You never get cinnabar deposits going very deep. We could even try digging. I suggest we're systematic. I'll take this area, say from here, over to—'

'It's pouring with rain,' Kate protested. 'I'm not digging in the pouring rain.'

'The dark's comin' on, sor, and we've no shovel for diggin'. I never knew it was to be a diggin' expedition. I'd say—'

'Here, I've a couple of hammers, you might not have to dig very deep,' Henry said, dropping to all fours in the swampy grass. 'It's usually not far under the surface. Trouble is (*dig, scrape*) there's all this rubbish first. Ridiculous. See, if anyone had asked I'd have said (*hammer, dig*) the most likely places for cinnabar would be Wicklow and Donegal and wherever, out west—Connemara, that right?—places you have gold quartz veins, and up north in the Antrim basalts probably best (*scratch, hammer, scoop, scoop*) of all, but in fact when you look at the surveys we're (*scrape, prod*) igneous right here, we must be, though I'd have guessed north of the Galtee area would have been more probable, I don't mind admitting it. Ridiculous. Try over there, why don't you, I haven't looked there, and work this way, towards me.'

Hammer, hammer.

Kate stood flabbergasted. Rain was falling steadily, darkness was closing in, and there in the bog on hands and knees, scrabbling and rootling like a pig after acorns, kneeled this man with the minus-twenty lenses and bandaged nut, this oblivious nincompoop, this snuff-sniffer, this pink freckled wine merchant who couldn't be allowed loose without a copper to take care of him, jabbering nonsense, enraptured by God only knew what, thrilled, hammering at the soggy soil of Ireland and effecting, so far as she could perceive through the gloom, extraordinarily slow progress. What else did he keep in his barmy satchel? Spare bandages? Sandwiches for nights spent digging the bog? Kate turned up the collar of her tweed jacket. But for this buffoon she would have been at home in Ennis, hours ago, whole and dry and drinking hot tea at the turf fire.

Thinking of him a little?

The notion was so preposterous that Kate uttered an involuntary snort.

'Beg pardon, miss?' Garda Griffin queried.

The lady seemed to be talking to herself. This did not surprise him. They were a queer oul' pair altogether. The big fella all the way from Canada, losin' his dog, his life in direst peril; the Miss snooty, then jokin', only a feather of a thing she was, but with a harmonious voice for a song, and sayin' it was none of her doin' bein' shot in the foot, but there was no knowin' with women, and no smoke without fire. If yez made yez bed yez oughta lie in it, no moanin', Garda Griffin believed. He picked up a fragment of stone and compared it unconfidently with the lump which he still held in his hand. Funny colour, both of 'em. Gob though, he'd stay dumb, he'd not be taken a second time! She'd be after coddin' him again given the chance, and it wasn't his job, findin' the sinnerbar stuff. His job was guardin' the minin' fella.

Garda Griffin looked all round him, circling through three hundred and sixty degrees, watchful, listening, guarding. Holy Mother, but 'twas gettin' to be a black oul' night!

'I guess it's a bit pointless,' Henry said, and gave a gentle grunt as he straightened his back. 'I'll come back in the morning with a spade. It's here all right. Here's another piece from the drilling.' He was kneeling upright, shining his torch on a sample of cinnabar which he held six inches from his glasses. 'Any luck, Kate?'

No answer.

'Kate?'

Silence.

'Kate—hullo? Where's Kate'

'Dashed for shelter, sor.'

'Hey, it's wet!'

Henry and his bodyguard ran through the rain and squeezed into the workmen's hut where Kate stood huddled with her collar up, leaning on her stick. There were no seats for sitting, even had there been space. The hut was squatter and fractionally roomier than a bathing-machine, and appeared to have been constructed from tarpaulin, corrugated iron and three or four planks. A sweater, stiff with dirt, hung from a jagged outcrop. Two empty beer bottles lay on the ground, on one of which Kate reposed her tartan foot. Rain rattled on the corrugated iron, swept through the doorless entrance, and into the hut.

'We can't stay here all night, let's run for it,' Henry said.

'Ready, steady, go,' Kate said.

'Hell, I forgot. Sorry. It's just that, well, you seem so

mobile. Look, would you let me carry you? We—'

'I've been carried, remember? Carry Mr Griffin. It's his turn.'

''Twill ease if we're patient,' said Griffin.

'Look, see?' The rain forgotten, wounded feet forgotten, Henry shone the torch on his second cinnabar find.

Griffin, risking all, reached forward with his own discovery and held it beside Henry's.

'That's it,' Henry said. 'Where'd you get it?'

'In the grass.' Griffin struggled for a facial expression pitched between a scientific aloofness and the nonchalance of the gifted amateur. He failed. He beamed. His chest swelled. Tunic buttons quivered and glinted, the horizontal creases creaked. He whispered, 'Is it the sinner-bar, sor?'

'Right. What do you notice about it?'

''Tis pink.'

'I wasn't thinking of that. Still, good. We usually say it's cochineal-coloured, kind of. Now, what else?'

He reminded Kate of an enthusiastic coach, a schoolmaster, striving to stir thought-processes in a backward pupil. She borrowed from him the third sample of cinnabar and turned it over in her hand, observing. Henry retrieved from the policeman the original sample. Cramped in the flimsy shelter, each of the three prospectors now held an apple-sized hunk of dirty, roseate rock. Kate and the bodyguard examined and pondered. Henry watched them eagerly, smiling, directing the flashlight's beam on first one sample, then the other: the tutor, waiting with his betas and alphas.

''Tis dirty here,' the guard said at last, 'and shiny here.'

'That's where the drill sliced it,' Kate said.

'Yes, yes,' said the tutor, 'what else, though? What about the weight?'

This, Kate realized, was for the jackpot, and while she considered the question of weight the guard leaped in and said, "Tis heavy!'

'Ah!' said the tutor.

Alpha.

'Heavy as lead,' elaborated Griffin.

'Heavier,' enthused Henry. The men stood toe to toe, jiggling in their hands the cinnabar, weighing it. 'It's one of your spot checks. The specific gravity's eight, lead's only seven-point-five. Gold's anywhere from fifteen to twenty, of course, but there's nothing higher than gold. No, so far as I can remember cinnabar's eight, compared with, say, around three for most minerals, though the earth's surface as a whole is five-point-five. Compared with three for water. Take say a carbon mineral like ordinary coal which—'

'I don't see why it's so special if it's just for thermometers,' interrupted Kate, who didn't want to take coal, or another word about specific gravity, which she did not understand. 'Is it terribly rare? You're so delighted about it.'

'I am?'

Henry put his sample in the satchel. Dead true, I am, he told himself. Who wouldn't be? Cinnabar in Ireland. The local memoirs would have to be rewritten, the maps redrawn. Not every day did a geologist stumble by hazard on the totally unexpected. Serendipity, that was the word. Not once in ten years.

Mercury in a Cork meadow. Quicksilver.

Defiant, he took the sample out of the satchel, and with it a double-lens magnifying glass. Outside the hut, night had arrived. Henry handed the flashlight to his bodyguard to hold, opened the times-eight lens, and through it scrutinized the pitted pink surface of the ore.

'Quite rare,' he said. 'The biggest mine's at Almaden, Spain, it's been worked for two thousand years. Some in Tuscany. And near Trieste. The Greeks and Romans worked those. Peru, Mexico, a little in the States. But that's about it.' He breathed on the lens and polished it on his elbow. 'Until now.'

'Can I keep mine, sor?' Garda Griffin asked.

'Sure. Vermilion, I forgot that. Mercuric sulphide gives you vermilion.'

'It's beyond me,' Kate said, and she craned her neck towards the black outside to see if the rain were abating. 'I always thought it was runny stuff.'

'How, runny?'

'Did yez t'ink it came up from a mercury well?' asked avenging Griffin, grinning mightily at Kate. 'In a bucket?'

'I did not!'

Closing the times-eight lens, Henry opened the times-fifteen and rescrutinized. 'It's the only metal which is liquid at ordinary temperatures. Is that what you mean?'

'I suppose so,' Kate said, sulking.

'It's highly volatile, and of course the vapour's poisonous, we had a lab technician go down with mercury poisoning.' While the bodyguard trained the torch's beam, Henry scratched earth off the cinnabar with the rim of the magnifying glass. 'Crazy thing is, the medicines that helped pull him round were part mercury for all I know. The pharmaceutical industry uses it. Metal and electrical industries. Scientific instruments. Most of your electrical switches.'

''Tis a useful class of stuff,' Garda Griffin said, nodding.

'Detonators,' Henry said in a puzzled voice.

He was about to consider why detonators puzzled him when he heard the click, alien and mechanical, outside the hut. They all heard it.

Garda Griffin barged past Henry into the night and rain, the clerks Nagel and Gallone, and an exploding point-blank pistol.

CHAPTER XIV

Some twenty seconds later, running, Henry decided that this first gunshot must have been a practice, a limbering-up, a flamboyant gesture into the sky as from a happy cowhand loping into town at round-up's end. Had the gun been aimed, something or someone must have been blown apart.

Twenty-five seconds later, Henry concluded that, aimed or not, the surprise would have been if anything had been hit. Such was the momentum with which his bodyguard had cannoned forth, one shoulder buffeting a wall of the hut, a size-fourteen garda boot demolishing a prop in the opposite wall, that even in the act of sighting their Colts the cowhands must have believed themselves in the dust and mayhem of a cattle stampede. As he hurtled, Garda Griffin had raised the same banshee howl as once before, at the Kilkelly Castle Hotel, when Inspector Mulligan and Superintendent O'Malley had entered without knocking.

'Aweeeeeeeeeeeeeegh!'

Grounded amid collapsing planks and corrugated iron, thrashing at tarpaulin, Henry had found Kate's tartan foot, then some other part of her, then a hand. When he opened his eyes there was nothing to see but night. He struggled with Kate. The Griffin howl and echoes of the gunshot were still in his ears when a burst of bullets, sustained, as from an automatic weapon, introduced a finger of light into the blackness.

Henry ran with Kate bouncing like a rolled carpet in his arms. She was alive and fit, or reasonably fit, because she punched the air, and himself, and uttered the incoherent noises of hysteria. The din of a third burst of gunfire was sufficient to make him stumble.

He careered on, detecting for the first time that he gripped the carpet upside-down, back-to-front. The legs flailed high before his eyes, the fists were beating at the back of his own legs. He tried to keep from thinking of Garda Griffin and to concentrate on making his strides long and floating. Once he had seen on television part of a football game in which the commentator had repeatedly eulogized the 'long and floating' strides of someone or other.

He fell in a crater, or trench, something shallow and mud-filled, as a renewed clatter of gunfire burst against his eardrums. Kate tried to squirm away but he held on. Which way was the car?

Someone, not Kate, not himself, shouted. The gun fired again. The racket rocked his head. Henry wanted to shout, 'It's me—Butt! Why me? I've done nothing!' He rose to his feet and blundered forward.

'Poomdow—poom*dow*!' Kate sobbed, flailing and beating.

Henry ploughed blindly through grass. She'd lost her walking-stick, he realized. Thank God, or I'd be clubbed to death.

She was clinging to her handbag, though, pummelling it against his running legs. The satchel at his hip flopped and bounced. A tree advanced and he changed course, skirting it. The miracle would be if now he might run head-on into the waiting garda car. Henry started to pray for miracles.

He lumbered rather than ran, angled forward from the waist, mouth open, glasses about to vault from his nose. His stride was not long and floating so much as irregular and drowning, impeded by hostile grinning limpets which tugged at his shoes each time they hit the sea-bed. He trampled across what appeared to be a path, a stony track, but though it might have led to the car a self-preserving instinct cautioned him to ignore it, to slog forward. He staggered through a field of cabbages or potato-stalks, something knee-high and inhibiting which exuded a clammy smell.

Kate had ceased flailing and was holding tightly to his haunches. His ankles burned. They were weak ankles, he had always had weak ankles, at school Snotty Carter had excused him from the steeplechase because of his weak ankles, but he had not been permitted to slide out of either the mile or long-jump, and had come last in both. His arms were parting from their sockets.

I've weak arms too, Henry thought, gasping.

As he sidled through a gap in a hedge, into pasture, a renewed outburst from the gun, a stereophonic bleat in the night, brought him fatuous hope. They were pursuing, whoever they were, but if they kept on shooting they would wake people up, there must surely be someone to wake up, they would alert the police with their shooting, and run out of ammunition, and lose heart, and turn back and surrender. A hole of some kind tracked across the pasture and into Henry's line of flight. He plunged both feet into the hole and fell headlong, discarding Kate.

Unburdened, immobile in the long grass, Henry watched with stupendous relief as Kate crawled away from him on hands and foot, dragging after her the wounded tartan and the handbag. He had tried to rescue her but in so doing had only made her a target for bullets. He imagined he heard her call, 'Horse,' but as this made no sense the misheard word might have been 'Gorse.' She was being stabbed by gorse and was sending back a warning.

Or 'House'? Had she spotted a house?

'Give me a leg,' she moaned.

She was being indistinct to the point of incoherence. What she meant, Henry reasoned, was 'Give me a hand,' or alternatively, 'Give me a leg up.' She was standing on her good leg, the tartan leg was bent and lifted, and her arms clung to the back of a horse.

'Don't be silly,' Henry said, standing.

'Whisht! You'll frighten him! Help me up!'

Henry grasped Kate's waist and hoisted. She swung the tartan foot over the horse's back. Henry stretched his arms across the broad back and jumped. He fell winded on the horse's back, behind Kate, and felt an onslaught of blows about his head and shoulders. The horse was jiggling up and down. Kate had twisted round and was thumping him with a small fierce fist.

'Geroff! You're too big! You'll flatten him.'

The horse was moving forward as it jiggled. The combined factors of its slippery wet surface, the rising and falling motion, his lack of grip, and the thumping from Kate, caused Henry to slide sideways. He slid as in slow motion, aware that he was about to fall off but unable to understand how to prevent it. Kate was now thumping with her handbag. The animal decided to stand still and wait. Groping for something to hold to, saying nothing because there was nothing to say except 'So long', Henry fell with a squelch into the pasture.

'It's no use, I can't ride without reins,' Kate said, dismounting. 'He has a halter but no reins.'

'Would,' said Henry from a recumbent position in the grass, 'my bandage do?'

Kate protested but accepted the bandage which Henry unfurled from his head. She knotted its ends to the halter, then with an eager one-legged jump succeeded in remounting.

'Come on then,' she said, aloft. 'Get up.'

'Me?'

'Hurry up. He'll give us a start.'

'I'm too big. You said so.'

'He's huge. We'll manage. He's well trained. Quick.'

Henry patted the beast's muzzle. 'No, you go. We'll separate. See you back at the hotel.' The horse lifted its head and squirted two jets of hot cumulous breath which misted Henry's glasses.

'Get up, will you,' Kate said.

Henry moved in the direction of the animal's stern, reached across hindquarters as flat as a ship's deck, and sprang. The horse started forward with Henry aboard, but crosswise on his stomach, like a bolster.

'Get astride, can't you!' Kate called out. 'Have you never ridden?'

'Hell!' cried bouncing Henry into the night, watching the rushing black grass below.

'Always playing the fool!' Kate shouted.

Proceeding from the prone to the astride position on the cantering horse, behind Kate, but refraining from using Kate as a post to hold to and climb up, was, Henry found, the most alarming athletic manoeuvre of his life so far, an act of faith and contortion which would, he suspected, cause him to awake trembling in later years, should he survive into later years. When finally he sat astride he realized the horse was motionless, nuzzling a gate. Kate was telling him to get down and open it, and shut it again when they had passed through.

'We could walk now,' Henry said, having accomplished all this.

'He'll carry us miles,' Kate said. 'He's strong as a horse.'

Henry held Kate's waist as the heavy Irish hunter bore them bareback along a boreen, then in a canter across meadows and fields. They thought, each independently, of Garda Griffin, but made no mention of him.

The guns were silent. The rain eased. Kate and Henry found and investigated a cottage but it was in darkness, locked and abandoned. They rode on, Kate clinging to the bandage, Henry clinging to Kate. He had a compass in his satchel, but no torch to see it by. The satchel flopped on his back. He had never ridden before, and what amazed him was that he was so high above the ground. It's all a matter of balance, he assured himself, shifting his grip to Kate's hips.

Horsewoman Kate balanced like an acrobat. Uneasy about squashed crops, she allowed Dobbin to pick his way across a potato field. Which way, she wondered, were the Galtee? What was she doing riding through the night with the pink man, wounded, fleeing from guns? The horse waded through a stream.

'Simple,' Henry said, regarding the water below, 'hardly over the rowlocks.'

'Fetlocks,' Kate said.

'Sure.'

In the next field sheep lumbered to their feet. They were on high ground. Kate patted and halted, with blandishments, Dobbin. 'Look,' she said, pointing. 'Down there.'

'I've seen.'

Turned in the same direction, Kate and Henry watched the distant twin sparks which could only be car headlights.

'Is it moving?' Kate said.

'I don't think so. They've been there the last five minutes. Maybe half an hour.'

'Can they see us?'

'No idea.'

'They might be parked. I'm sure they're not moving. Perhaps they've burst a tyre.'

'Yes.'

'Or a poacher.'

'Could be.'

'Wouldn't they call out if it was?'

'You don't think it's the guards looking for us?'

'I don't know. Do you want to go and see?'

'Not much.'

'Shout then.'

'Better not.'

'We can't stay here. They might be coming up the hill.'

'I know,' Henry said. 'We'd better go. Start her up. Gee up, Silver.'

'He's not Silver, he's Dobbin,' Kate said, urging Dobbin forward.

'You're very sure he's a he,' Henry shouted into the wind. Kate's hair had become unpinned and it streamed in his face. 'How do you know he's not a filly?'

'Don't be asking me why! Ask your parents!'

A Grand National hedge hurtled towards them. Dobbin veered away, found an opening in the hedge, and plunged through. The headlights were nowhere to be seen.

'Do you know how long we've been riding?' Henry shouted.

'How long?'

'Over an hour.'

The horse trotted. Kate turned and looked at her passenger. 'You've mud on your face. You should see yourself.'

Henry said, wiping mud, 'You've something above your cheek.'

'My eye.'

'Under your eye.'

'That's where the hut fell. And personal abuse isn't very chivalrous for a girl who's teaching you to ride to hounds. Grip with your knees now.'

Kate turned front and they were off once more at a canter, through bog, then on to a road. They looked both ways along the road into the night. Rain was falling heavily again.

'How about it?' Henry said.

'You say. Let's risk it.'

'Okay. This way?'

'All right.'

They had trotted twenty yards along the road when the car came. They heard it before they saw it, a drone submerged in the rustle of pouring rain, but the decibel count ascending, exalting, instant by instant, until with blazing headlights and a crescendo of combustion engine the green sports car raced towards them. The glare illuminated Henry clinging to Kate's waist, Kate struggling to turn Dobbin towards the ditch which divided the road from the field. Dobbin jumped the ditch. The car's engine momentarily expired, then roared again, reversing, aiming the headlights, and then was vanquished in a bedlam of automatic gunfire.

Dobbin galloped across the countryside.

In time, he slowed. Kate allowed him to walk. Without speaking, shocked, swallowed by rain, drooping, Kate and Henry rode on. Farmland, fields, sleeping cows, rain. Kate cried a little. Henry, eyes closed, tried not to lean upon her. He looked about him, hoping to give an impression of alertness for danger, and said:

'What's that?'

'What?'

'There, by those trees.'

'It's like something for bus passengers to wait in.'

'That's us. Bus passengers. We're not moving from here till the Greyhound arrives.' Henry, climbing down from Dobbin, seemed to be all legs. 'Off you get. We've had enough.'

'But we're nowhere.'

'The best place.'

He took Kate's hand and helped her down. Then he swatted Dobbin's rump. 'Hup! Off! Vamoose!'

Dobbin trotted into the night.

'Horse de combat,' Henry said.

The bus shelter which was no bus shelter, there being no road, was smaller but more lovingly constructed than the collapsed hut at the cinnabar site. A carpenter, perhaps a joiner even, had put it together with joints and joists, a board floor and a roof. There were no seats : simply the upended shoe-box of a hut, open on one side. Outside Government House in Ottawa, reflected Henry, two sentries, two bearskin-hatted Mounties, could have occupied it. Maybe three, though not with horses. On the floor were cigarette ends but no bottles.

'It'll have to do us till morning,' Henry said. 'Sit on my jacket.'

'I don't want your jacket.' Kate sat huddled in a corner. 'I suppose you didn't bring a Thermos?'

Henry dropped his satchel by Kate's handbag, eased his bulk down beside her, and put an arm round her shoulders. Her head moved on to his chest. She said :

'I've a confession.'

'I absolve you.'

'No, seriously.'

'Okay.'

'I'm not really a housekeeper.'

'That's different. What are you?'

'Nothing much. Tired.'

Henry wondered what time Ireland began to grow light. Kate, eyes shut, inconsequentially counted in her mind her savings. It was as effective as counting sheep.

CHAPTER XV

On a road north of Carrigann drove a garda car, head-lamps thrusting two cones of light into the night and rain. The windscreen wipers swept with a muffled clicking. In the rear seat O'Malley, grim, said:

'Time?'

'Three-ten,' Mulligan said.

'Roadblock ahead, sir,' said the driver.

Ahead twinkled a light. Two police cars barricaded access through a crossroads: as was the case at all junctions in the Carrigan area. Arclights and a generator for the Ivernia site, and still more police cars, more police, were arriving from Limerick and Cork. O'Malley's car halted at the roadblock. The driver wound down the window. A sergeant, cape glistening with rain, stooped and saluted.

'Anything?' O'Malley said.

'Not this way, sir.'

'Let us through.'

'Sir.'

O'Malley's car drove through and on.

'Time?' O'Malley said.

Inspector Mulligan peered at the luminous dial of his watch. He was unable to fathom why the time should be so vital. Speed, yes, but the precise hour of the night, what did it matter?

'Three-fif—'

'Bad luck to 'em,' O'Malley said.

The headlights of an approaching car dipped as they drew closer. The car slowed and was almost stationary when Superintendent O'Malley's car passed. Faces glowered through the windows. 'Guards,' said O'Malley's driver.

'Miners, thugs, foreigners, people,' O'Malley muttered. 'Bad luck to 'em all.'

'They'll need their luck out there tonight,' Mulligan said, staring through his side window.

'Sorry for them?'

'Butt and the woman.'

'If I'd my way, you know what? I'd give them machine-guns, all of them. Then I'd lock them in a cupboard and let them get on with it.'

'We have to find them first. They might have got on with it already.'

'They might so, God willing.'

Mulligan opened his mouth, sought with a fingernail among the molars, and surprised the fibre of roast beef which had been trapped there since his sandwiches-and-Fanta supper at Egan's. He understood but could not quite share his chief's sweeping, un-Christian feeling, and wondered if there might not be a seasoning of role-playing. When all was said, he'd known Griffin better than the Dublin man had. Extracting the fibre, Mulligan decided no, no role-playing, this feller means it, and God help JZA 622 when we find her.

Garda Feeney, busybody, had found Griffin. After the night's first feast of gunfire had been heard and debated, Feeney had gone looking with Paddy Boland, who farmed most of the land north of the village. By the time O'Malley and Mulligan saw Griffin the rain had washed him clean. Half of his head had been shot away, another salvo had ripped the front of his tunic from the Kerry bull chest.

The windscreen wipers swished. The guard beside the driver took a crackling, unenlightening call over the radio. In the back, commanding the manhunt, O'Malley sat slouched in a corner, hat pulled down, eyes shut. Inspector Mulligan glanced at his chief and thought: 'Tis the violence unhinges him, violence breeds violence. Mother Mary and Joseph, the way he's acting we're not done with the violence yet!

Non-violent Flynn, co-proprietor of the Carrigann Park Hotel, arranged himself for sleep on a mattress in the dining-room alcove. With new arrivals every day accommodation was desperate. The big Canadian and the wounded lady didn't seem to have shown themselves for the night, and he'd been tempted to recover his old room, now the wounded lady's room. But 'twould have been an embarrassment her returning in the dark, as likely as not, and locating in her bed a co-proprietor. The alcove was grand. A fine type of curtain and a view to snatch your breath. At closing-time in Egan's, the lights doused, the door barred, and the real drinking starting up, rumour had gone round of guns to the north.

But he couldn't be bothering his head over jinks like that. Tomorrow there'd be a million things to do keeping the guests' comfort up to standard, and a hotelier needed his sleep.

Cousin Cooney trod through sodden undergrowth: brambles, briars, bracken, burdock, nettles, crabgrass, ragweed and oxeye daisies. He wore gumboots, a raincoat over his pyjamas, and carried in both arms a grocer's carton announcing, '*An Bord Bainne*. Finest Dairy Products.' The carton was heavy and Cooney trod with stealth, taking his time, lifting high each gumboot then depositing it with care so as not to be tripped by brambles. Bulldoze this lot and we'd have the grandest orangery in Munster, it'd come under the six-year plan, ruminated Cooney. His toe clanged into a furtive oildrum, camouflaged by grass and thistles. He stepped over the oildrum and bore east, away from the stables (West Annex), through a less vegetable area dominated by mud, on to a crunching cinder path, and through an arched gateway in a wall. On this side of the wall the view was of savagery run amok, or would have been had it been visible in the darkness. Here was primeval jungle: abandoned, dank, grotesque and impenetrable. This was the walled garden. Cooney penetrated by a secret route known only to himself and one other (Flynn), a track hacked out by native labour (themselves) using machetes (or sticks) two days previously. Waterfalls from nudged vegetation tipped over Cooney. Soggily he penetrated. Against the far wall of the walled garden leaned the shed that once had housed gardening implements, fertilizers, stacked boxes of seed potatoes, and now, as Cooney advanced, started to shiver from the sudden yelping cacophony within. Cooney slipped the catch, opened warily the shed door, and tossed into the interior the carton. Seventeen starving greyhounds fell on the spilled bones, tripes and roughage. Cooney slammed the door and retreated through the jungle.

That would hold 'em till morning, just. He'd have to have a proper sit-down talk with Reaney, the butcher. Trouble was, now the greyhounds had been shifted out of the way of Mr Nosey Inspector, getting to them with food and drink had become a destroyin' class of a hike.

At the Kilkelly Castle Hotel at the same appalling hour of three fifteen a.m. slept barman Brian Mahoney in his narrow bed in the south turret. He had, as routine, placed his trousers under the mattress to preserve their crease, hung on a coathanger the malachite-green jacket with KCH on the breast, and locked the door against the assistant chef, who lusted after him.

In narrow beds in adjoining cubicles under the rafters of the same turret slept the assistant chef, smelling of Guinness, the head waiter, smelling of whiskey, and other staff, each with his or her idiosyncratic perfume. On lower levels, watched over by flouncing damsels and laughing, plumed conquistadores, slept guests.

Air Commodore Reginald Cowley (Retd), an insomniac, did not sleep but sat propped against pillows sipping whiskey and reading *Essen and Aftermath, 1944. The Role of Air Power in World War Two, Strategy and Tactics,* Vol. IV, by Gp. Capt. T. G. Summerville, DFC, OBE. Gertrude, his wife, slept by his side and dreamed of cross ruffs, jump bids, pre-emptive bids, squeeze play, take-out doubles, informatory doubles, redoubles, overtricks and yarboroughs.

William N. Michelson, another insomniac, lay in bed studying the telephones section in *The New York Times Encyclopedic Almanac*. His home was in Greenport, Long Island, and he looked forward to being back there. Meanwhile, he was mesmerized by statistics: the USA had 103,752,000 telephones, more than five times as many as the next country (Japan), though Sweden followed the USA in respect of telephones per 100 population, and when it came to telephone conversations per person gabby Canada had the edge over his own country, and third, oddly, came Iceland, while Britain, which had more telephones than anywhere after the States and Japan, didn't appear to use them.

In their separate rooms slept two other American golfers, and a fourth, Dr Langer, had finally fallen asleep after imagining distant echoes of gunfire. Guns did not disturb him. What nagged was the prospect of being awakened by a soft voice requesting that he come and lend a professional hand in sorting the dead from the dying and the dying from the merely shaken, as inevitably must happen if recent form were a guide. The golfing foursome had time calls for six forty-five a.m. and an early nine holes, weather permitting, prior to departure for Portmarnock. Thence Scotland, and a week at Gleneagles.

Ramsey Gore's room was empty. Not normally an insomniac, the manager sat in his office poring over accounts and licking the tip of a ballpoint. Bookings were down. After eight years he had had his bellyful of Ireland. He would sell and return to the only sane spot on the earth's surface, London. The question was, when? Timing was the difficulty.

Two other empty rooms, recently vacated, and even more recently filled by guards with dusting-powder and plastic bags, had belonged to the guests Nagel and Gallone.

Nagel and Gallone sat in the green sports car, parked with extinguished lights beneath a clump of firs. Dawn would not hold off forever. They were aware of the manhunt and time running short, yet their actions were methodical, measured. They were a team. Nagel fitted a fresh clip into his automatic rifle, Gallone kept his eyes on the sauntering horse with the bandage-reins. Wordlessly they climbed from the car and closed its doors.

Dobbin, grazing round the rim of a bunker, looked indifferently towards the sound of closing doors. He had wandered some distance from the scrubby hillock where he had been vamoosed. His sweat had dried on him.

O'Malley blasted out of the bunker with a chip-shot which raised the sand like a Nubian simoom. The white ball soared, dipped, bounced on green grass, rolled, teetered, then dropped in the hole. The crowd screamed and threw their greasy lunch packets in the air. He had won the American Open.

Why American? O'Malley wondered, opening his eyes. Why not the Irish? And how come he had managed to beat Christy O'Connor, in his day still as supple as a willow?

Evidently they had just passed through another roadblock. The car gathered speed along the empty road.

O'Malley frowned.

'Is there a golf course round this way, John?'

'No. Only Kilkelly.'

The slouched square shape of the Superintendent stayed for a little while slouched. Then it lurched forward and up.

'Romantic Ireland, how are ye!'

'Pardon?' inquired Inspector Mulligan.

'Get to Kilkelly,' O'Malley ordered, thumping the driver on the shoulder.

'We skirted Kilkelly a while back,' Mulligan said. 'This road—'

'Kilkelly!'

CHAPTER XVI

'It's,' Henry heard a woman say, 'Sunday.'

He did not immediately open his eyes. He knew he was in the mystery shoe-box, paralysed with cramp, and that the thin shabby light pressing on his eyelids indicated the night was over. When he raised his eyelids he would be back in the world, a re-entry he was happy to postpone. The trouble would start when he tried to move his limbs.

Cinnabar, he remembered, with stirrings of interest. He had found cinnabar, they couldn't take that from him. Unless of course while he lay there they found him, those gunmen, if they were still looking. How long would they look?

Had they killed Griffin, that boy, really killed him?

Henry inhaled and shifted a leg, testing for numbness. The lumbar area, where he had fallen from that most egregious horse, seemed especially tender. He levered his torso off the board floor. The right knee had suffered more than lumbar territory. Something had entered the knee and was trying to chisel a way out.

'Sunday,' Henry echoed.

He sat flexing the knee and hooking his glasses over his ears. Besides being damp his clothes were disorganized, and he rearranged and buttoned. Kate, at some stage of the night or early morning, had moved away and was sitting a few inches from him in the doorless entrance of the hut. She had repaired her own clothing and to a courageous extent, with tissues and cosmetics, her face. The black hair hung down, pinless but combed. The tartan foot was basted with mud, the grey tweeds were crumpled but ordered. Beyond her, outside, Henry saw more grey. The morning was misty, not yet fully light. He looked at his watch but it had stopped. He looked up and smiled at Kate.

'Hullo.'

'Good morning.' She was smiling back. 'You're a deep sleeper.'

'Did you sleep?'

'I did.'

Before shyness could take hold he leaned forward and kissed her good morning. Her mouth being wide, moist, open and lipstick-flavoured he continued kissing, hugging the underweight body to him, enveloping her, feeling her fingers moving over the back of his neck, a little lower than the bandage, then digging into his neck. Abruptly they were gone, and her hands were against his chest, pushing him back.

'You're an avid man, Henry Butt!'

'I am,' Henry agreed, playing for time while he recovered his breath, 'I am, Kate Kennedy, I am, I am.'

'You're a mess too, look at you. First time I saw you you were pink as soap. All scoured and polished.'

'I'll be scoured and polished again, you'll see. Just show me a bath.'

'They've fifty baths over there.'

'Where?'

'Kilkelly Castle.'

Poking his head out of the hut, Henry saw daffodils. For a moment he saw nothing else. The frilly toy trumpets were a yellow blanket which had been set down not far from his nose, flanking a path, and spread out over a shallow hillside. Here and there fir trees spiked the blanket, and farther down the slope where the land grew level the yellow was holed by a pool of green, and slashed across by a green road. Beyond the green road were scattered misshapen yellow rugs, but green dominated. There were bushes of darker green, trees, craters of sand, and distant green pools, each with a pin like a surfacing periscope, from which drooped a red pennant. Then the mist.

'The hotel?' Henry said. 'Are you sure?'

'You could see it five minutes ago but the mist came down. Watch a while. I think 'tis lifting.'

They held and caressed each other's hands while they watched. Kate said:

'I knew all the time it couldn't be a bandbox.'

'Sorry,' Henry said. 'This morning you'll have to spell it all out. What bandbox?'

'This thing. You said it was a bandstand for a two-piece orchestra.'

'You said that. I said it was one of those hideaway places you shoot duck from.'

'Shooting . . .'

They were silent. The mist hung in horizontal layers, dissolving, solidifying, dissolving again.

'Anyway,' Kate said, 'it's for golfers.'

'I can see that. Why?'

'When it rains.'

'In Ireland they must be quite an industry.'

'Very droll. Look now, can you not see a bit of a turret?'

'Yes. Kate, listen. I've got a proposition.'

'You've made plenty of those already.'

'When?'

'Half the night. My proposition is we go to the hotel and borrow a bathroom. Two bathrooms. You can carry me if you like.'

'No, listen. I fly back to Canada tonight.'

'I know.'

Kate disentangled her hands. She opened her handbag and started hunting.

'Come with me,' Henry said.

'To the airport?'

'To Canada.'

'Canada? It's the jolting from the horse, it's deranged you.'

'I mean it. Think about it. No, don't think about it. Do you have a passport? Hell, are there regulations? You don't need a visa, I'm certain, not the Irish.'

'What visa? You're making no sense at all.'

'Dammit, if you won't, I'll stay here.'

'Goodness, you're a person of impulse! I'd never have thought you were like this.'

'First time.'

'You don't think I'll believe that. Is this an immoral proposition you're making?'

'If you like. Marry me. Will you?'

Marry? Kate, having closed the handbag, opened it again. Keys, cosmetics, tissues, mirror, diary, pencil, wallet of savings, Kilkelly invoice, letters, several toffees, ticket for the Irish Sweep. She rummaged. Her mind had shut like a scallop. She heard the man beside her say:

'Will you?'

'I couldn't do a thing like that.'

'Yes you could. You must. Kate, listen, please. Are you listening? I love you.'

'Ah, not at all.'

'But I do.'

'You do not.'

'I tell you, I do. Dammit, I know whether I love you or not.'

'You only think you do.'

'Of course I think I do. That's what I'm saying.'

'There, see? It's infatuation.'

'It is not goddam infatuation!'

'You're swearing at me,' Kate said, and began to cry.

She let him take one hand while with the other she groped for a paper handkerchief. He began talking in a quieter, rational tone, like a suffering, martyred pundit on television trying to penetrate the stultifying ignorance of the interviewer. Love was unanalysable but you knew

it, surely, when you'd got it, he explained. He accepted
that this was perhaps sudden, certainly unexpected, but
not precipitate, by no means, and when you analysed it,
and here was a matter open to analysis, why should it
be unexpected, why, her being so warm and giving, and
himself, well, he was no movie star, but he enjoyed life,
he was reliable, travelled a bit, useful income, never been
in prison, healthy, or healthy until he'd come to Ireland, and no reason why he wouldn't be healthy again
after he'd left. See, love simply had to be accepted, or
rejected, and if accepted, love in many instances went
with marriage, and why not in this instance? There'd be
details, naturally there'd be details, they were from different countries for a start, different cultural and envir-
onmental backgrounds, but if the premises were valid,
the conclusion must follow, the syllogism would stand.
Not that logic and love, he imagined, were subjects
ideally suited to each other.

Henry fell abruptly silent. Fiddling with Kate's fingers
he stared gloomily over the frivolous daffodils. Somewhere a thrush had begun to boast. Kate, mopping her
eyes, said :

'You know nothing at all about me. You don't even
know if I can cook.'

'That's okay, I can cook. What else?'

'I'd not let my husband do the cooking!'

'So you cook. What do you cook?'

'Different things,' Kate said, cagey, suspicious of traps.
She moved closer as an arm encircled her. 'Mutton?'

'Mutton. Well, okay. You don't see too much mutton
in Canada.'

'Why ever not?'

'I guess it's more beef, steaks. Lamb, of course. Pork.'

'I like mutton.'

'Sure, who doesn't? Don't worry. We might be able to have it flown over.'

'I wish you'd be serious.'

'I wish I would. Seriously, does that answer the mutton question?'

'I never imagined I'd be asked to live where they don't have mutton.'

'Look, we've solved the mutton. I didn't say they don't have it. I said it was unusual. Like buttered caddis fly. Have you mastered the art of French cooking?'

'I have, in a flash.'

'I guessed it.'

'D'you like Irish Stew?'

'Mutton?'

'The secret's putting whole potatoes on top of the stew so they take in the fat. They absorb it.'

'That secret should have been kept secret.'

'Why?'

'People don't know how to keep secrets these days.'

'You're mocking.'

'It's because you keep talking about food. What's the breakfast menu down there? In the hotel.'

'Rashers. Anything. We ought to go.'

'You haven't said yes yet.'

'Yes what?'

'You know what.'

'I've not said no either.'

'You've said nothing else. No to me, yes to mutton.'

'Are you giving up?'

'The Butts never give up.'

Kate laughed. The pink mottled head, cropped hair freed from its turban, was very close. She could have counted the freckles. Instead she sought out a patch of cheek uncluttered by mud and kissed it. Henry blinked through gibbous spectacles.

'That's yes?' he said.

'That's a girl has to have time. Listen, I only met you yesterday.'

'Day before.'

'Palm Room, seven o'clock.' Kate sighed. 'Then you offered me supper and never came back. Then you had me shot in the ankle—'

'Calcaneum.'

'—then last night, oh, I can't think about last night. Truly I can't.' After a moment, Kate said, 'Are you insured?'

'Imperial Life, Sun Life, Toronto Mutual. You'll be worth a lot of money when I'm gone. Way things are going, that could be any time.'

'Don't. There are so many things. I mean, like, well, what about children?'

'What about them? Love children.'

'And blood tests?'

'Yes. Love blood tests.'

'You're useless. And religion—what about that? Would you take instruction?'

'Certainly I would. No problem. What in?'

'I'm a Catholic.'

'I'm a sort of Catholic myself.'

'You are?'

'Ask my parents. Tomorrow.'

'Is that the truth?' Kate pondered. 'I'm not saying it matters.'

'Father O'Flanagan wouldn't agree.'

'Father Fahy. He would not either. He's the old school.' When Henry said nothing, Kate added, 'My dad was an optician. He died in January.'

'Share mine,' Henry said.

After a moment with nothing to say, and still having nothing to say several moments later, Kate and Henry held each other and kissed. The thrush blew a symbolic tremolo, gobbled chromatically, flung in a bravura arpeggio, rounded out the arpeggio with a brisk roulade, then flew ostentatiously into a sky changing from ash to milky-blue.

The mist had dispersed. Beyond the lake, on the far side of the golf course, stood Kilkelly Castle, a child's cut-out of sham turrets and galleries. On the gravelled forecourt people and cars came and went; an unlikely sight for the hour of morning, thought puzzled Kate, especially Sunday morning. On the golf course a thumb-sized foursome trundled golf carts. Like routed, unhorsed hussars returning from the Plains of Abraham, Kate leaning for support on Henry's arm, Henry limping from knee and lumbar pains, the pair hobbled from the hut and through daffodils.

They had progressed two dozen yards when the shooting broke out again.

CHAPTER XVII

'They're the guests, the ones who flew past us in the sporty car, I'm sure it's them.' Parting with her hands the eye-level daffodils, Kate craned forward. 'Wait while I see their faces.'

'Just don't let them see yours.'

'Wouldn't you say it's the same two who shot me?'

And Bodyguard Griffin, and damn nearly us, and cracked my head in the men's room, brooded Henry, who wanted nothing beyond a helicopter, fitted with bath, which would winch Kate and himself up and away, first stop Toronto.

'D'you imagine that's Dobbin?' Kate said, focusing on the horse with dangling bandage which grazed far off, beyond the lake, in the region of the fourteenth green.

Watching the gunmen's backs, Henry whispered, 'They must give up, they must, they don't have a chance.'

Henry and Kate lay prone in daffodils. Prone in sand a hundred yards in front lay the Common Market clerks : swart, expensively dressed, uncommunicative except for their banging guns. Youthful, yet old enough for their own turn at being shot to pieces. Their bunker, a sandy pit guarding the seventh green, gave cover from the front but not from behind. They lay with their backs to Henry and Kate and fired in the direction of the hotel.

Strung out along a fairway, clubs and carts abandoned, the American golfing foursome were running for the hotel. Kate recognized Dr Langer. An older, plumper golfer, too round for running, peeled away from the fairway and into the rough, where he tripped and fell. He picked himself up, stumbled on, but fell again and stayed fallen, invisible in long grass.

'Nagel and Gallone!' Through a loudhailer the voice of O'Malley echoed indistinctly across the golf course. He gave Gallone a soft G and two syllables. 'Jettison your weapons and come out with your arms up! Do you hear me?'

'They're not,' Henry said, 'going to tell you whether they hear you, you nut.'

'Where is he?' Kate said.

'Can't see. I think behind one of the cars.'

'I can't see anyone. What were those two shooting at? It can't be just Mr O'Malley on his own.'

'There—see! There's one!'

A blue garda, crouching low, sprinted forward across the grass in front of the forecourt. One of the bunker pair fired. From the hotel issued a return of firing. The running garda vanished behind a fir tree.

'God!' Kate murmured.

'Do you hear me?' crackled O'Malley electronically. The query hung like a kite in the dawn air. 'Nagel and Gallone, this is your last chance! Fling out your armaments!'

Gallone, or Nagel, had turned on his side in the bunker and was reloading a gun.

'I don't like it,' Kate whimpered, sinking her head into daffodils.

'Don't worry,' said Henry, who didn't like it either, but attempted officer-like to spread sang-froid among the men.

'Let's get back to the hut.'

'Wait.'

Henry peeked over the yellow blanket's surface. Two more police were running forward, then vanishing behind trees. The bunker pair did not fire.

'Let's get out,' Kate appealed. 'We could creep back up there, then into the wood.'

'Suppose they saw us, it's us they're looking for.' Though no one was in earshot, Henry whispered. 'Keep your head down.'

'Keep yours down.'

'It's all right.'

'It's not, it's awful! Can't we get out!'

'It's okay, it can't last long.'

Miserably, Henry contemplated logistics. If the police came forward, shooting, and the gunmen were winkled from their bunker, and back, the gunmen's line of retreat would be back and up, through the daffodils where lay Kate and himself.

A more formidable hazard would be the guns of the cops. Could they shoot straight? If they rushed the bunker would they shoot at anything they saw moving?

Henry felt sick. He breathed noisily through his mouth. If he'd had his bandage, unravelled, off-white, fluttered aloft as a distress signal, would it have invited or diverted police bullets?

'The guards haven't guns,' said telepathic Kate, weeping. 'They don't carry guns in the south.'

'These do.'

'No, they don't, not in the south.'

'I'm sorry, they do. You heard them.'

'I think they have to sign for them.'

'So they've signed for them.'

'Please, I'm going. Help me up.'

'Stay down!' He wrapped an arm round her. 'It'll be over in a minute. They haven't a hope.'

'You keep saying that. Where are they, the guards, if they're supposed to have all those guns?'

'Somewhere. Half a million of them if it's like Canada.'

Because a cop had been killed, Henry believed, though to have said as much would only have added to Kate's distress. Propped on one elbow, he watched a man in a raincoat crawling with a rifle up an unmown bank at right-angles to and fifty yards from the bunker. A car engine started revving in the forecourt.

'This is your last chance!' O'Malley stereophonically offered, generous with this second last chance. The car from the forecourt weaved between trees at five miles an hour, heading in the direction of the bunker. 'You have ten seconds!' O'Malley crackled. 'Do you hear? Ten seconds! Do your own counting!'

Kate sank her head among the daffodils.

Three . . . four . . . five . . . Henry counted to himself.

He reached seven before he realized he was counting and that he had already reached seven. Behind the bald policeman in the raincoat crawled a younger man in a thornproof sports jacket, gripping a pistol big enough to bring down an aircraft. Then four uniformed guards on their bellies.

Eight . . . nine . . .

Nagel, or Gallone, put his head above the rim of the bunker, then bobbed down. They've no more bullets, deduced Henry.

He watched: the gunmen, the creeping flanking party

led by Inspector Mulligan with a rifle, the car emerging from its cover of firs and starting across a fairway towards the daffodil blanket and the bunker. One of the gunmen glanced sideways, bringing his face into profile. He wore glasses. His upper canines and incisors caressed and soothed his upper lip. His chin was streaked with mud: souvenir of the night's games, Henry supposed. The gunman looked front, over the bunker's rim. In each hand he held a revolver.

Fourteen . . . fifteen . . . sixteen . . .

The other gunman, a classless clerk with pomaded hair and an automatic rifle, stood upright in the bunker and fired a burst at the approaching car, shattering the windshield and causing the car to slew in a half circle. Inspector Mulligan, kneeling, shot the clerk through the temple. The gunman in glasses fired once, a token, in the direction of the flanking party, leaped from the bunker, and careered down the incline, away from the ambush, away from Kate and Henry.

The man in the thornproof jacket fired his pistol. The gunman ran in a zig-zag, head down. Thornproof-man fired again.

'Save it!' Mulligan roared, racing past the bunker in pursuit.

Thornproof-man and uniformed police accompanied Inspector Mulligan. Mainly in the hotel area the scene was suddenly aswarm with guards, but also in the outback, the golfing and parkland recesses of Kilkelly, guards surfaced from coverts, bushes, bunkers, hollows, singly and in groups, and converged on the fleeing man. From the woods higher up charged two constables, and through daffodils close to Henry and Kate.

The gunman, tacking as he ran, altered course to avoid the lake. In altering course he headed towards police. He changed course again, racing the other way round the lake.

'Surrender yourself up, Gallone!' O'Malley crackled ethereally, the command bursting godlike out of a baby-blue sky. 'Don't be acting the bloody eejit, man!'

The running gunman (later identified as Nagel) fired a shot at a garda uniform. Someone among the scattered horde fired back, whereupon the gunman slowed his pace to a stroll. He stopped strolling and stood still, arms hanging down. Still holding his revolvers, he sat on the grass. He toppled on to his side by the lake's edge as the first guard reached him.

Deep in daffodils, sweating, regarding with horror the remote, milling figures, Henry waited for O'Malley to make an announcement. He had the ghoulish impression of a whistle and full-time. Except for an arbiter's proclamation of the final score, the match was finished.

'It's over,' he told Kate.

There was no announcement. Henry fancied he saw O'Malley, a square, hatted figure, striding across the forecourt.

On the edge of the fairway below the bunker, attendant guards thronged round the prostrate garda car. Towards the car ran two more guards carrying a stretcher. In the bunker, the clerk killed by Mulligan lay cruciform, eyes staring, sand coating his careful, unguented hair. The dropped gun was partially buried in sand. Guards jogged up the slope towards the bunker.

Henry prised himself on to his knees and waved to the guards. Kate, trembling, sat up and began foraging in her handbag. One of the guards who hurried towards them was a sergeant whom Henry believed he had met somewhere, though he could not recall where. Into a walkie-talkie the sergeant requested a stretcher for Kate. Kate protested that she could manage. Sergeant Byrne demolished the objection with an airy backhand gesture.

'There's stretchers running to waste, Miss. They have 'em stacked up like deck-chairs on a beach.'

Before a stretcher arrived, O'Malley came for Kate and Henry in his own car. He had stopped to see for himself the crippled garda car and its occupants. He had looked briefly in the bunker. Now his driver negotiated the fairway, the rough, and parked in the daffodils. With O'Malley was a policeman sparkling with stars and braid, and a lugubrious detective who sucked a toffee. O'Malley and the braided guard helped Kate, then Henry, into the car.

'You'll have to walk,' O'Malley told the toffee-eater. 'Pass the word if you get wind of Gore.'

In a low gear, wary of bog, the car headed back towards Kilkelly Castle. Kate clutched her handbag and stared unaware at the bristly back of the driver's neck. She returned to the world only when Henry's hand alighted on hers. They smiled at each other before looking away again. Henry's free hand rested on the satchel on his hip. He had anticipated a more genial, even congratulatory reunion with the forces of law, but his anticipation was misplaced, and understandably. O'Malley, in grunts and monosyllables, confirmed that Griffin was dead.

Somewhere a fire-engine or ambulance brayed with monotonous energy. The starry policeman received on the two-way radio a call concerning Ramsey Gore. Evidently he had been missing. When guards had started closing on Kilkelly, and had been rewarded by the dawn discovery of JZA 622, then by a sighting of Nagel and Gallone themselves, the non-appearance of the ubiquitous manager had mildly mystified. When the action started, Gore's continuing non-appearance piled mystery on mystery.

Gore, the radio-message revealed, was dead too, impaled on the end of a golf-pin on the third green, this green, Henry gathered, being on the north side of the hotel, away from the action. The manager had enjoyed his own ultimate piece of action, away from riff-raff, presumably stumbling on Nagel and Gallone in advance of the guards.

Unless, O'Malley hazarded, though he thought this improbable, Gore had connections with Nagel and Gallone, and thieves had fallen out.

"Tis maybe callous but my feeling about Gore,' O'Malley said, 'is that he's a class of an anti-climax.'

CHAPTER XVIII

Inspector Mulligan, looking for Superintendent O'Malley, intruded his burnished pate into the Palm Room.

At the bar, Brian dealt spoons into saucers. Though he had slept through the holocaust he understood that a crisis was afoot; that his boss, for instance, among others, had been mortally gathered. Brian had entered the spirit of crisis by wearing a roll-neck jersey in place of the barman's jacket, so giving himself an improvised battle-stations air.

In scarf and bathrobe, like a boxer reliving younger, punchier days, Air Commodore Cowley sat waiting for tea and information. Beside him, Gertrude wore slacks and headscarf.

The golfing foursome were absent.

The English bridge pair, having acquired all the information they needed, had retired to their room to pack. Inspector Mulligan had passed them in the lobby.

The last pair he sighted, sitting by the same window where he had seen them meet two nights ago, were Miss Kennedy and Mr Butt. Their faces were washed but their clothes ravaged. The Canadian had discarded his head-bandage, and the red of his curly cropped hair appeared to have faded for want of oxygen.

Mulligan hesitated and was lost. They had seen him. A porter in an apron said, 'Pardon,' and squeezed past into the Palm Room, carrying the tea-urn. Inspector Mulligan walked across to Kate and Henry, attempted a reassuring smile, and said:

'Are you all right now?'

'Fine,' Henry said, 'thanks.'

'Thank you,' said Kate.

'I was seeking Mr O'Malley,' Mulligan said.

'He's finding us transport to Carrigann,' said Kate.

'He said he'd be ten minutes,' Henry said. He wondered what had become of the Inspector's rifle. Had it been handed in with exchanges of dockets and signatures until the next time? 'He went to look at, er— Mr Gore.'

'I heard about that.' Inspector Mulligan sounded as

excited about Gore as had the Superintendent.

'He said he'd be ten minutes.'

'Good, good.' Inspector Mulligan shifted his weight on to his other foot. 'That's grand then.'

No one had anything further to add. Mulligan, uncomfortable, prepared to say, 'Excuse me,' and depart, but he missed his chance because Henry, clearing the air, said:

'We were in the grass above the bunker, higher up.' He wondered whether he ought to congratulate the Inspector on his aim. 'We saw you.'

'I saw you,' Mulligan said. 'You did well to stay clear. Anyway, it's finished.'

'Thanks be to God,' Kate murmured. Looking through the window she spied in the forecourt, among the confusion of official vehicles, an opportunist taxi, charcoal-coloured except for yellow mudguards. Billy Dunne, peaked cap squarely on his head, was shining the rear window with a cloth. I'll walk, Kate thought. I don't care if it is twelve miles.

'Couldn't you stay on now, if you wanted?' Mulligan suggested to Henry, half an eye on the closing of the file, which would require interviews, eye-witness accounts, signatures, documentation. 'No need to rush off.' No need for bodyguards, the Inspector considered. Police bodyguards were suddenly in short supply. 'Cancel your flight reservation?'

'I thought I might.' Henry glanced at Kate. He had contemplated moving back to Kilkelly. He would not mourn his alcove at the Carrigann Park Hotel. Presumably the Kilkelly Castle would stay open, though managerless. Kate was studying a snagged fingernail. Henry said, 'I must cable Toronto.'

'Do it from here,' Mulligan said.

'Yes,' agreed Henry, looking round, as though for cable forms.

'Would you like a cup of tea?' Kate asked.

'No, no,' said Mulligan, shifting to the other foot.

'Three teas,' Brian said. He sorted cups of tea off a tray and on to the table.

'Ten minutes, you said?' Mulligan said.

'He's here now.'

Watching from the window, Henry had spied O'Malley, the toffee-eater and the braided guard stalking across the forecourt. The braided guard stalked on while the other two disappeared into the hotel entrance.

'Will I fetch another?' Brian asked the Inspector.

'You'd best. He likes his tea.'

"'Tis a thunderclap about Mr Gore,' Brian said. To Henry's relief the barman's expression registered awe. Here at last was someone not totally nonchalant towards violent death. Brian said to the Inspector, 'Shall the staff just carry on as though he wasn't here.'

'Please yourselves. There'll likely be questions so don't chat about it.'

'It's going to be a deprivation.'

Brian shunted back to the tea-urn leaving Henry questioning whether the deprivation was Gore's demise or the command not to chat about him.

O'Malley came into the Palm Room with the toffee-eater. Ignoring Kate and Henry, he asked Inspector Mulligan to see if he couldn't round up Dr Langer. The doctor, O'Malley believed, should at least take a look at Gore, if only for the sake of the reports. Last seen,

Dr Langer had been ministering to one of his golf buddies. A wounded guard in the wrecked garda car had not been wounded after all, O'Malley informed Mulligan, not in the sense of having been struck by a bullet; he had been merely stunned, somehow, and was now recovering. Another guard, however, a Chief Inspector from Limerick, had been shot in the calf, it was rumoured by a bullet from the gun of a certain sergeant, also from Limerick. (Final count, computed Henry, two gunmen dead, against two dead guards in the wrecked car, a dead hotel manager, a stunned guard, a guard shot in the calf, and something or other ailing one of the American golfers. If you went back in time and added in dead Harvey and McGrew, dead Griffin, Kate shot and himself occasioned a crack on the head, the final sum would be a casualty list around a dozen strong. All, Henry suspected, for cinnabar. From here on, O'Malley told Inspector Mulligan, it looked like mopping up, finding relatives, telephoning, writing reports. The forensic lads were having a lurid affair with the green sports car. A priest was on his way. Any moment the Assistant Commissioner was due from Dublin. The Press would descend. Reception was trying to reach the assistant manager, a Mr Jepson, on holiday in Ibiza.

O'Malley sat, tilted back his hat, and appropriated a cup of tea. As Mulligan left, Brian arrived with more tea. O'Malley would swoon, Superintendent O'Malley insisted, if Brian did not bring biscuits. O'Hara, the toffee-eater, helped himself to tea. O'Malley introduced him:

'Inspector O'Hara will drop you off at the Carrigann Park. Is that the name—Carrigann Park? Whenever

you say. You'll be ready for a change of clothes. Wherever did y' spend the night? Down a zinc mine?'

'On a horse,' Henry said.

'A horse, was it? We've an unclaimed horse by the
lake.'

'When will you want to hear about it?'

'You could give me the outline.'

Henry did so: the excursion to the Ivernia site and
the finding of cinnabar, Garda Griffin charging the guns,
the night ride on horseback. Now Gallone and Nagel
were dead he might stay on, convalescing, he said.
Working, if the drilling got under way again, because
unless he was mistaken the work which lay ahead would
be stimulating. Would the police need him for help
over details?

Kate spooned sugar into her tea. She never took sugar
but vaguely believed it contributed a medicinal quality.

'I'd been hoping for a chance to look over the site
with you,' O'Malley told Henry. 'What's cinnabar? I've
heard of that.'

'The ore of mercury.'

'Hermes!'

Henry disregarded what he imagined must be a Gaelic
oath. 'I'm as certain as I can be without a laboratory
on tap,' he said, digging in his satchel.

'Hermes,' said O'Malley, slapping his knee, 'is the
Greek Mercury. Sweet Jesus, I'm thick! Mercury is
Roman. And I was tryin' to tell myself 'twas inconse-
quential.'

'Oh?' Henry said, defeated. He took from the satchel
the remaining hunk of cinnabar.

Sipping sugary tea, Kate awaited elucidation. Brian

was back with biscuits, a bottle of wine, and glasses. He set down the biscuits in front of O'Malley, the wine beside Henry.

'Pomerol,' Brian whispered. 'I saved it for you.'

'Well, thanks.' Flummoxed, Henry eyed the bottle. 'Not now though. Thanks anyway.'

'It's the nice one, the one you ordered. See, I stuck the cork back in to stop the gas escapin'.'

'Yes, I see, thanks a lot. But we couldn't just now.'

'I'm thinkin' the Superintendent would turn a blind eye,' Brian said into Henry's ear in a whisper which susurrated round the Palm Room and caused the turning of all heads not already turned. ''Tis not licensing hours, I'll grant you that, but you're a guest in a manner of speaking, wouldn't y' say?'

'Leave it stay and get about your duties,' Inspector O'Hara said, and helped himself to a ginger-nut.

Scorned and rejected, Brian moved muttering away. O'Malley drove his teeth through a circular biscuit surmounted by a centrepiece of sugared, bluish-pink flannel. He picked up the cinnabar.

'Cinnabar, eh? Is it valuable?'

'Yes,' Henry said.

'Will there be plenty?'

'I'd guess so. Depends what you mean by plenty.'

'And what do you do with it, with mercury, apart from thermometers?'

'Detonators.'

'Is that so? Detonators.' Superintendent O'Malley ruminated. Why detonators should be a more curious and provocative commodity than rugby balls or cottage cheese, he was not sure, but he surmised that probably it was. 'Detonators, is it?'

'All kinds of scientific instruments, medicines—'

'Would you excuse me?' Kate smiled apologies, scooped up her handbag. Her mottled geologist was gathering steam and she had heard it all. Moreover she felt queasy from sugar. How long were they to sit and jabber and herself a scarecrow? Men had no sensitivity. She protested, 'No, don't move, you carry on, I'm just taking a walk in the air.' But they were pushing back their chairs, as she knew they would. O'Hara was pushing back and simultaneously selecting a chocolate-digestive off the plate. The Superintendent and her massive man were arranging lunch at Egan's, noon, then a trip to the site.

O'Malley moved with his tea into Henry's chair by the window and watched them go: Inspector O'Hara indecisive about offering support to the hobbling woman, the woman lop-sidedly leaning, holding to the Canadian's forearm. Sliding the Pomerol out of the way, the Superintendent wrote in a notebook: *Cinnabar—mercury. Detonators. Thermometers. Medicines.* He looked at what he had written, then out of the window. O'Hara was holding open a car door for Miss Kennedy and Mr Butt.

Superintendent O'Malley drank tea, summoned additional biscuits, suspended judgement on the painting of red circles at the stern of the room, and cerebrated. Interpol would furnish a dossier on Nagel and Gallone. They were not miners, they were hoodlums, and they'd be known. But who'd put them up to it? Miners? A rival mining company, Australian possibly, who knew about the cinnabar, or who didn't know about the cinnabar

but for whom the zinc and lead prospects were enough
of a green light? From what he'd read in the newspapers,
Australian mining companies, one or two of 'em, were
not above a class of jiggery-pokery. The Ivernia drill
had been smashed as a warning. The gun under
McGrew's window was a loose end, but there were often
loose ends. Some in the fullness of time would be knotted,
others tucked out of sight. He hadn't a particularly
tidy mind, more a wandering one, and he'd no objection
to a few loose ends.

Inspector Mulligan came into the Palm Room with
Dr Langer. The Superintendent signalled to them with
a finger, then to Brian.

'How's your friend—Michelson, is it?' he asked the
doctor.

'Heart attack, second this year. He'll be in bed a
month.' Dr Langer wore his Aran jersey and carried a
familiar black bag of potions and surgical implements.
He sat on the arm of an easy chair, paunch sagging
above the belt of the topaz slacks. 'There's something
else, if you're interested. I was telling your Inspector.'

'Gore,' said the Superintendent.

In his mind O'Malley saw the manicured green and
the late manager, spreadeagled, the pennant of the golf-
pin flapping in the breeze. He did not know what had
gone wrong but it had to concern Gore, a nuisance
in death as in life.

'Dr Langer says,' said Mulligan, 'he's not been dead
more than an hour.'

'At the most,' Dr Langer emphasized, looking at his
watch.

All three men were studying their watches. Mulligan

looked at Superintendent O'Malley and said:

'An hour ago Gallone and Nagel were holed up on the golf course.'

'So,' O'Malley said, 'we have at large a golf-pin maniac.'

'It wasn't the artists in the bunker.'

'Right.' O'Malley stood up. 'No one leaves the grounds. And the fewer in the better.'

'Trouble is,' Mulligan said, then hesitated.

'What's the trouble?'

The policemen were striding from the Palm Room. Dr Langer slid from the arm and into the seat of the chair, glad after all he was a doctor, not a policeman. He looked round profitlessly for Brian, who had deserted to the kitchens to sulk and eat rashers and eggs.

In the lobby, Mulligan said, 'The trouble's Mr Butt and Miss Kennedy. They've already left.'

'I'll believe most things but not them. What're you suggesting? They were above the bunker, you saw them.'

'What I mean is, I mean I'm not sure we've got very far in this business.' Mulligan and O'Malley stepped into the forecourt. Guards began scurrying, pretending to be useful. A detective in conversation with the night porter was making notes on an envelope. 'Butt,' said Mulligan, 'has no one to look after him. O'Hara's dropping them both then coming back here. I don't like it. If—'

'Get a couple of cars down to Carrigann fast!' O'Malley thought: I'm growing old and slow, they'll have to retire me. 'I'll phone. Go yourself. And don't let that Butt feller out of your sight—or the woman.'

O'Malley charged back into the hotel. Before Inspec-

tor Mulligan could remember which of the guards in
the forecourt had been issued with firearms, the Superintendent was back in the hotel entrance, shouting at
him.

'John! If he's cancelled that flight, uncancel the
cancellation!'

CHAPTER XIX

Inspector O'Hara dropped Kate and Henry outside the
Carrigann Park Hotel then continued into the village
in search of breakfast. He wanted to be alone. After
the night's waking, stalking unreality and the climactic
rumpus of the dawn (a tale which would be worth many
a pint in Mooney's come pension times, and come
next week for matter of that), he wanted a half hour by
himself, unwinding over fried sausages, tomatoes and
the sports page. More urgently, he needed to replenish
his confectionery supplies. There was no rush to return
to Kilkelly. Ryan's he noticed, looked a likely boutique
for the flakey-bars, and was open. Curse of God, he
cursed, steering round a gawping dog which deserved to
be run down, and one day would be, if there were justice.
A witch in bedroom slippers, slopping along the pavement clutching a plastic bag of milk, threw him the evil
eye. He noticed Egan's and recalled the name: a useful
spot for hospitality, he felt confident, if they could be
roused at this hour on a Sunday, or any other day, come
to that. Would they do a fry-up for a Dublin garda faint
with hunger? O'Hara parked, locked up, and walked

back towards Ryan's grocery only seconds before col-
leagues at Kilkelly tried to reach him on the car radio.

In the Carrigann Park Hotel, Kate locked the bathroom
door and looked round for a chair or hook. Seeing
neither, she placed her towel and accoutrements tidily
on the floor. The bath, a lidless enamelled sarcophagus
on brass paws, was the highest bath she had ever seen,
almost as high as herself. I've need of a ladder, she
thought, rising on her toes, then looping over to put in
the plug. She turned a tap. Instead of water there issued
a croak as from some imprisoned denizen struggling for
release. Then gathering in sound and velocity, like a
transcontinental express approaching a station where it
had no intention of stopping, came a high whine which
caused the tap, indeed both taps, to tremble. The whine
intensified to a shriek, and the whole bath began to
shudder. Abruptly, but with no loss in volume, the
whistle changed to a zoological trumpeting. The trumpeting became in turn a staccato bleat of astonishingly high
decibel count, causing taps, bath, and the floor under
the brass paws, to quake in frenzy. Kate had met such
baths before. Gingerly yet resolute, like a householder
probing the entrails of a troublesome television set, she
reached out and tuned the tap, gambling on a half-twist
to starboard. There followed an impressive silence. She
dealt the tap a karate chop, whereupon scalding water
exploded forth. Droplets bounced and flew, steam thick-
ened like soup. Kate fell back against the wall. She took
off the muddied tweeds, sank in her slip to the floor,
and started on the unravelling of the tartan foot.

Kate Butt, she said to herself. Then she said the name

aloud. 'Kate Butt.' She repeated it, aloud, trying to detect in the words a chime, a euphony.

Crouched over an open suitcase in his alcove, Henry listened to the banging of the hot water system. Dammit, he thought, with a glance at the figure on the mattress, if they don't wake him it won't be for want of trying. Though at his back the dining-room was empty, the tables bare, the hotel was alive with noises: plumbing, creaking, frequent footsteps, slamming doors, a ringing telephone that no one answered, clinking of cups and saucers, muffled pop music from a transistor. There were people too. In the entrance hall he had passed two men with briefcases, editors or stockbrokers with lost, unbreakfasted faces. He believed he had seen Cooney, a bucket in each hand, disappearing down a corridor.

The alternative co-proprietor slept under an army blanket, mouth open, vest buttoned up to his chin. Henry ferreted through the suitcase. He had sorted out a comprehensive change of clothing. All that was required was the waterproof pouch of toiletries.

'Henry,' whispered a voice.

Odd, thought Henry, that Flynn should use my first name, and he peered at Flynn, who slept. Henry twisted further round and looked up at a Canadian, not an Irishman, looking down.

But for protruding, lobeless ears which hung on the sides of his head like question-marks, the man's appearance was almost abnormally nondescript: eyes, nose, mouth, chin, medium-brown hair above, medium-build body below, size nine shoes, knee-length tan raincoat. Ears apart, and even the ears never would have warranted mention in any text-book on physiognomy, the intruder was unremarkable. He would have been even more unremarkable had he been less dishevelled. Dried mud on the shoes and raincoat left Henry wondering whether this person too, whom he knew only slightly, might not have passed the night riding horses and sleeping rough. The darker stains on the raincoat, on the cuffs particularly, Henry identified as blood.

'McGrew,' Henry said, and so far as his part-kneeling, part-squatting posture allowed, he sprang forward.

Henry, horrified, had aimed to spring past McGrew, but misjudging he struck some part of a leg with his shoulder in a foul but effective tackle. McGrew cried out as he spun sideways, and Henry careered through the dining-room, along the passage, and three at a time down the wide central staircase. Flynn stirred in his sleep, uttered 'Jaze, we will, we will of course, don't fret y'self,' and slept on.

In the entrance hall, Henry looked back. McGrew, limping and grimacing, was taking the stairs four at a time. Henry, shoulder tingling, sought for guards, but the only figure in the entrance hall, turning the pages of a pink newspaper, was a guest who smiled nervously at him, then at McGrew on the stairs, believing an Irish jape, a category of Gaelic rite, possibly historical, almost certainly regional, native to north Cork, and now being enacted for the amusement of guests. Henry ran down steps from the front entrance and along the drive.

He no longer doubted that Danny McGrew was a murdering maniac. For the last dozen hours, since discovering the cinnabar, he had suspected. Until McGrew was found dead, suddenly there had emerged good reasons for believing him alive. If McGrew had not himself murdered Harvey and Griffin and Gore, he had paid the two golf-course gunmen to do so, and to do the same for Henry Butt. He had become criminal, presumably, because of the quicksilver deposits and their potential in cash. McGrew was, or had been until twelve hours ago, alone in his knowledge of the mercury. To preserve this status, Harvey, Butt and any subsequent geologists, had to be disposed of.

How McGrew imagined he could indefinitely continue killing geologists, Henry failed to comprehend. For the moment his problem was in reaching the village to avoid becoming the latest victim. The blood on McGrew's cuffs, if it was blood, suggested a recent killing. Gore? Henry pounded along the drive, encouraged only in the thought that he was leading a maniac away from Kate.

How fast could McGrew run? Only five or six minutes of hard running to Carrigann's main drag, and people. McGrew was cutting across the field.

Henry's first notion was that the madman intended dropping into hiding in the grass and shooting him with a rifle, at leisure. Only McGrew carried no rifle.

A pistol? How far did pistols fire?

Henry's second guess was simpler, and accurate. McGrew was taking a short cut. If he could climb the six foot wall before Henry reached the road, McGrew would be first in the road, blocking it, barring access to the village.

Breathing like sandpaper, Henry steamed towards the gateless stone pillars and the road.

The road was empty. On this spot, Henry remembered, Kate had been shot. He found himself treading on tiptoe along the road in the direction of Carrigann, a cartoon caricature of stealth, arms jutting like wings, head and trunk swinging forward, back, forward, back, the husband returning to domestic base after a night of inebriation and riot. A three-minute dash ahead he could see the war memorial and the lilac-painted corner shop of Carrigann's main street. Advancing catlike towards him along the top of the wall, he saw McGrew.

They eyed one another. Henry noticed stains on McGrew's shirt front, as on the raincoat cuffs.

'Henry,' McGrew called, and looked downward for a place to descend.

Henry took a step backward, turned, and lumbered out of the starting-blocks with the grace of a bull moose. His shoes slapped flatly on the tarmac as he ran past the pillared gateway to Carrigann Park. Would McGrew shoot now?

'Butt—hey, stop! You gotta go!'

Henry had gone, galloping for his life in the wrong direction, away from Carrigann, onward and deeper into green, interminable spaces. We've all gotta go, he silently agreed, and the words rotated in his mind, repeating themselves, keeping rhythm with his thudding feet. He glanced over his shoulder at McGrew in pursuit. I'm twice his size, I'd have gone forward, fought him, if he hadn't had the gun, Henry told himself. If I could convince him his mercury secret was blown, that there was no more mercury secret, he might see the futility of more killing. But how convince? Puffing Henry believed flight preferable, in this instance, to discussion.

The road ribboned forward between mouldering walls stitched with ivy. On his right, Carrigann Park; to the left, woods. Towards him, distant but drawing nearer, incontestably in motion, drove a car.

Salvation. If McGrew did not fire first.

Henry ran along the crown of the road waving both arms in the air. The car, a grimy, cramped conveyance driven by a priest in a black hat, approached in a low gear, sounding its horn. At his side the priest had a passenger, another priest. The passenger-priest was gesticulating in Henry's direction. The driver-priest guided the car at Henry without slowing. Henry hopped out of the way and staggered backwards to the side of the road, brandishing both arms.

'Stop! Father—Fathers! Stop for Chrissake!'

The car grinded past at twenty miles an hour. Two black-hatted red faces dumbly, splenetically mouthed at him through closed windows.

'Stop!' Brandishing one arm in rage and frustration at the departing car, his free hand holding flouncing gold-rims in place on his nose, Henry ran back into the middle of the road. 'Papists!'

The car ceased hooting and continued towards the village. The rear fender was buckled where, Henry assumed and hoped, some persecuted citizen had booted it.

Where was McGrew?

The diminishing car apart, the road was again empty. Henry, panting in the road's exposed centre, sensed but could not see his compatriot. Behind the wall? Near where Henry stood the wall ended in a collapsed mound of mossy rubble. On the other side of the road, petering out in bog, the unknown of umbrageous woods. Ahead, open country. Ditches and low hedges cordoned off the

road from pasture. Another vehicle was approaching:
a lorry.

Uneducable Henry stood his ground with arms sema-
phoring. The lorry squealed to a halt.

'Will Mallow do you?' called out the driver, leaning
across the vacant passenger seat to wind down the
window and attempt to open the door.

'Yes!' cried Henry, already wrestling with the door
handle. 'Anywhere!' Between the two of them, each
twisting in a contrary direction, they held the door as
tight as a bo'sun's knot. 'The police!'

'What police?' shouted the driver, a lad with un-
trimmed hair. 'Where?'

'Let me up!' yelled Henry, wrestling.

'Will yous leave go o' the handle!'

'For Chrissake man, there's a maniac!'

'Damn true there's a maniac! Leave go!'

'Let me in!'

The youth succeeded in locking the door. He shifted
the gear lever.

"Tis the insurance, see? No hard feelin's, Dad!'

The lorry moved forward. Henry loped alongside,
breathing oil-fumes and calling through the window.

'For God's sake, let me up!'

"Tis the insurance policy coverage!' The lorry rolled
quicker. 'Yous have to mind the insurance!'

The lorry rumbled away, leaving Henry in command
of an acre of road.

If he could find it, the cinnabar site lay in the green
spaces, somewhere. He was to meet O'Malley there in
about four hours' time, after lunch. If he could keep out
of McGrew's way, hide, discover the cinnabar site,

meet up again with the cop . . . alternatively, if he could
beat his arms, take off, fly like a grouse to Shannon.

Henry started to run. Deeper into the green spaces he
puffed. More cars were speeding towards him. A convoy
of three or four. What was the psychology, Henry wanted
to know, for thumbing a ride in Ireland? Smile? Throw
rocks? Extend arm and finger with fluttering banknote
attached? Extend thumb and sing *The Rose of Tralee*?
The convoy hurtled towards him with no intention of
stopping. Barely had Henry backed into the ditch and
hitched into the air a tentative thumb than the convoy
was braking. Tyres protested. Four cars, Henry counted.
No, a fifth, a belated rearguard in the improbable form
of a white Cadillac bearing, Henry liked to think, perhaps the President of the Irish Republic.

Five cars, all halted for him. From the first spilled
O'Malley.

'God, man, you're all right so!'

Inspector Mulligan decanted from the third car. Co-
horts of blue gardai milled in the road.

'Is that the boyo—there!' shouted one garda, prompt-
ing all to look.

On the periphery of the pasture, running for the cover
of trees, was McGrew. He was no more than thirty
yards away, and when he turned his head to look back
towards the road the nondescript features were identi-
fiable. Henry opened his mouth to shout that, yes, that
was McGrew, but was forestalled by the double bang-
bang of a shotgun. McGrew dived headlong and disappeared in the grass.

Deafened, Henry looked from vanished McGrew towards the sound of the gun. In the road by the Cadillac

a man was lowering the gun (sixteen-bore) from his shoulder. His hair was black and lank, his jacket three hundred dollars' worth of tailored doeskin.

With Irish gardai substituting as gillies and beaters, Skipper Ogden was enjoying a day's hunting.

CHAPTER XX

'Suffering Jesus,' Superintendent O'Malley said.

'He was going for his gun, goddamit!' Skipper Ogden shouted. 'He's killed enough!'

'Did you tell Ogden,' demanded Henry, grabbing O'Malley by the arm, 'about McGrew?'

'Ogden, is it? All I know is he arrived at Kilkelly as we were leaving. Said he was your company president.'

'Did you mention McGrew?'

'I mentioned nothing! Is that McGrew?'

'Yes!'

Harassed O'Malley jerked free and started forward across the road, into the pasture. 'Come on!'

Pressing down the gravy-brown hat on his head, O'Malley trailed behind fourteen guards, lumbering like cattle towards the vanished man. Garda Feeney, busybody, was first to the spot. He crossed himself.

'Jesumarymotherogodprayfor—'

'Don't,' boomed Sergeant Byrne, trampling up, shouldering through swifter guards, 'touch him!'

'He's done for,' a guard said.

'Course 'e's bloody done for, so'd you be, yer great gom, and mind where ye'r treadin'.'

Garda Feeney produced a rosary.

'Who'll fetch the priest?' said a guard from the South Limerick Constabulary.

'Matter a damn about priests. 'Tis too late for priests.'

'Kinsella, fetch a priest,' said Sergeant Byrne. 'Tell Mr O'Hara what you're at.'

'Try Father Connor, other end of the village.'

'Mind now.' The shiny upturned bowl of a bald head thrust downward through blue uniforms. Squatting, Inspector Mulligan rolled the body on to its back. 'Anyone know him?'

Silence.

'See what he's got then,' panted O'Malley. He crouched beside the Inspector and started to feel through pockets of the tan raincoat. 'Mr Butt? Where's Butt? Bring Butt, one of you.'

'No gun,' said Inspector Mulligan, who had unbuttoned the raincoat and was tracing his hands over McGrew's jacket.

'He could have tossed it aside in an attempt to dispose of evidence, sir,' volunteered Sergeant Byrne.

'Start looking then.'

'Sir.'

'It's McGrew right enough,' O'Malley said, examining a passport. He passed the passport to Mulligan.

'That's it then.'

'That's it, John.' O'Malley sifted through McGrew's pocket-book: letters, credit-cards, driving licence. 'There's a letter to Marylene dated today. Isn't that the wife? Air ticket, Zurich-Dublin, return.'

'Zurich's where that Yank flew in from. In his own plane.'

'What Yank? Ogden?'

'Is that his name? Byrne's the only one spoke to him.'

'Byrne,' called out O'Malley, but Sergeant Byrne was a long stone's throw gone, aligning a grumbling pressed-gang of guards for the search through the pasture. 'Never mind, we'll have a word with Ogden. He's Butt's boss, he says.'

'He's a trigger-happy bucko.'

'He is. Where is he?'

O'Malley and Mulligan stood and looked towards the road, empty except for deserted garda cars and the white Cadillac. The sun, climbing, glinted on the car roofs. All police were in the pasture, three or four with Mc-Grew's corpse, most of the others a resentful, shanghaied search-squad now being organized by Sergeant Byrne. Garda Kinsella, trotting, almost at the road, had started to wonder whether he might have the loan of a car for Father Connor, or was he expected to walk?

'Kinsella-a-a-a-a!' Mulligan bawled, hands cupped to mouth.

Kinsella turned, identified the origin of the summons, and made a megaphone of his own hands. Respectfully he called, 'Hullo-o-o-o-oh!'

'Where's Ogden?'

'Who?'

'Og-den! The Yankee fella!'

'His name's Connor! Fa-a-a-ather Connor!'

'Ogden! Og-den!'

'Father Ogden is it?'

'Father Finnegan's Bloody Rainbow,' Mulligan muttered. He cupped his hands again. 'The car—the fella with the flash car!'

'Will I take the car?'

Inspector Mulligan closed his eyes. 'Good night,' he murmured.

'Leave him be,' O'Malley said.

'I'll ask for Father Og-den, will I?' Kinsella mega-phoned across the rippling pasture.

'Yes!' Mulligan shouted.

'John,' O'Malley said, 'where's Butt?'

'Where?'

'D'you see him?'

The two senior detectives surveyed the countryside.

'Jesus,' said Mulligan.

'You lot,' Superintendent O'Malley called at the search squad. 'Didja see Butt, any of you? Where'd he go?'

After a delay, a guard ventured, 'I saw him near the wall, that way.'

'When?'

'God, I was never one for the minutes. Five, would ye say? I was after t'inkin' he—'

'Find him! Four of you come with me! Sergeant, get after Butt!'

O'Malley, hand flat on the crown of his hat, started to run back across the pasture. Mulligan instructed a guard to stay with McGrew's body, then chased after his chief. He caught up.

'We'll find him all right, he must be here.'

'Sacred bleeding heart,' O'Malley panted, longing for Dublin and the files on the sweepstake fraud.

'They can't be far, either of 'em. We'll find 'em in two shakes.'

Inspector Mulligan was half, as it turned out, correct.

They were not far, either of them. But they were not to
be found in two or even twenty-two shakes.

The climbing sun percolated down through elm
branches and on to the curly head of Henry Butt, miner.
Not a great deal of sun remained by the time it reached
him for he lay full length in a ditch at the base of the
elm, and the mesh of vegetation above belonged not
merely to branches of his appropriated elm, or of other
elms in the clump, but to blackthorn hedge, gorse and
bracken. He lay stiff and still, not daring to lift his head,
heeding only the slow, crackling footfalls through twigs
and leaves of his Ivernia boss.

He should have run into the pasture with O'Malley,
holding his hand, but there had been no reason to do so.
Already weak with running, why should he have run
anywhere? In the moment he delayed, the guards had
scampered into the field, and Ogden had been walking
towards him, smiling. He had retreated from Ogden.
All he had had to do was shout to the cops; except that
Ogden would have shot him, as he had shot McGrew,
as he intended shooting him anyway, unless he could
get away, and rejoin the cops, over the wall possibly,
out of Ogden's aim for one minute, out of sight along
the hedgerow which separated the pasture from Carrigann Park. But the collapsed mossy extremity of the
wall had been too low for cover, farther on it was too
high for climbing, and when Ogden had snapped open
his gun to reload there had been no alternative but to
retreat fast along the road, Carrigannwards, then across
the road to the hedge, through the first gap and into the
woods.

Henry lay with his fist in his mouth in an effort to

muffle the sound of his breathing. He found it hard to judge whether Ogden's crepitating tread was closer or farther than a moment ago. The police were close, too, he had heard them shouting, but they might have been in another country for all the service they could be. One of them, Kinsella, was off to collect Father Ogden. That would be a tale for the Ivernia boardroom. If any Ivernia men were allowed to remain alive for tale telling.

Ogden's tread was silent, but Henry sensed his presence. The only sounds were cops calling to one another, a car engine coughing into life. In the fist not in his mouth he held his folded spectacles, a precaution against glint from the sun's rays.

The exiguous pool of sunlight on the dead leaves in front of his nose dried and perished as clouds moved across the sun.

'O'Malley, argued Henry, numb in his ditch, had not mentioned McGrew to Ogden. So how had Ogden known McGrew was around? How had he known McGrew, the running man, was McGrew? Someone had said the man was a boyo. That was all. McGrew was missing, presumed dead. Only he himself, Henry Butt, had known the man was McGrew.

Himself and Ogden.

A week ago, in Toronto, Ogden had never set eyes on McGrew. How, at the conference, had Ogden seemed to see McGrew, and all rock-heads? 'The bearded Klondike bear type'? Somewhere in the last day or two Ogden and McGrew had met. Probably. Ogden knew McGrew, knew he was alive, and required him dead.

Why?

Henry did not know. Mercury? Much of his theorizing about maligned McGrew—the paying of gunmen, the killing of Harvey, and Garda Griffin—could be switched to Ogden, effortlessly. The point was that Ogden knew and had shot McGrew. The shooting of Dan McGrew was the key. How had Ogden identified McGrew if he hadn't known him? Why not shoot, say, plainclothes Inspector O'Hara, if it were simply a matter of shooting? Why, were he merely hard-working, guiltless Skipper Ogden, magnate and gubernatorial candidate for the heroic Buckeye State, shoot anyone?

The pool of sunlight reappeared, and in it a restless woodland midge, a sylvan speck haphazardly flicking and cavorting. Henry removed his fist and breathed more evenly. By shooting shipmate McGrew, the Skipper had scuttled himself. Burned his boat. Not because he had shot a man; back home, maybe in the Emerald Island too, Ogden would have survived that on any of a dozen choice pleas from self-defence to defence of the realm before going on to demonstrate how Mad McGrew had been the scourge of Ivernia and a Communist. But because the act of killing the man he chose to kill showed he knew more than he should have known.

Blown it. Scuttled. Sunk with both barrels blasting.

Unless, of course, Henry realized, replacing the fist, starting to shiver, the double-barrelled gun could expunge clever Henry. Who else knew, or guessed, what Henry knew?

He lifted his head. Tree trunks, undergrowth, smells of leaf-mould and mushrooms, a random stippling of sunlight. A voice called, 'Feeney, the other side,' but distantly, from acres elsewhere. A car was approaching in a purring crescendo. Crazy cars, they'll be the end of me one way or another, Henry thought, putting on his glasses, hiking his head higher, risking all. He saw only gloom and stipple. The absence of a bang from Ogden's musket let him believe, for a moment, he was alone.

Then, from the gloom ahead, a metallic twinkle of sun on the gun barrels. Ogden was partially hidden by jungle, but what could be seen was turned away, watching the road. The car was about to pass. Henry had vaguely seen himself charging through the hedge and into the road for a repeat performance of the hitch-hiking act. When the car arrived, the safer, more profitable move seemed to be deeper into the woods, farther from the gun barrels. The car swept past, a flash of white Cadillac (Kinsella at the wheel) through the boscage. Henry trampled into the woods, elephant feet unheard (he hoped) in competition with the Cadillac's roar. The roar died to a drone. Henry gasped through curtains of scratchy flora. Abruptly the woods ended, and he was standing on the rutted frontier of a stubble-field.

They had not been woods at all; not, anyway, woods like Canadian woods. They had been little better than a coppice, a trivial spinney. Now, exposed, Henry faced farmland, and the foothills of the Ballyhoura. Should he go on, he would have liked to know, farther from cops and copse, putting space between himself and Ogden while seeking a furtive, anonymous road back to O'Malley? Or did he risk the quicker path to heaven or hell, back into the lethal spinney, and hide-and-seek between the trees? He could hear cars on the Carrigann

road. A police siren started to wail. Behind him, somewhere, was Ogden. In front lay only an exquisite view
and a tractor.

Not until Henry noticed the tractor did he realize
that his legs were water. Forwards or backwards, they
would not have carried him more than a dozen yards.

Light-headed, indefatigably a supporter of machinery
over horseflesh, Farmer Butt stumbled towards the
tractor.

CHAPTER XXI

Dear Marylene,
I am writing this at the Kilkelly Castle Hotel, not
actually in it but near enough, being as they say 'Per-
sona Non Grata'. They would suppose me a spook come
back to haunt them if they saw me, and I do not know
how long I have got, so please excuse the writing. There
is not much light because the fact is I am outside and
it is not morning yet. It is impossible to say how things
are going to pan out which is why I want to write and
tell you 'the low-down', which I am afraid is pretty low,
but what I am saying is I love you, you know that, I
will always love you 'come what may', and I am truly
sorry for anxiety and trouble I must have caused you.
I will not get morbid though because everything may
be all right and I hope you will understand and 'forgive
and forget' when I tell you.
As you see I am very much alive and intend to stay
that way—

'A miscalculation,' Superintendent O'Malley said.

'He spoke a bit soon,' agreed Inspector Mulligan, looking up from the letter.

They shared the rear seat of a garda car travelling in third gear up a back road behind Carrigann, looking for Henry Butt and the Yank with the shotgun. The heads of the two guards in front swivelled as they searched the landscape. A field away, three guards strode alongside a hedge, ritually poking its denser parts with blackthorn sticks.

'I suppose he might at that,' O'Malley said.

'Might what?'

'Come back and haunt them. McGrew. 'Twould be a diversion for the tourists—a ghost.'

'Two ghosts—wait, three. McGrew, Gore, Harvey. They'll be company for each other.'

'They can gas over old times. The merry days of slaughter. Go on with the low-down.'

'It's awkward reading. He cramps his letters.'

'You're doing grand, John. You've a delivery like a Thespian.'

A glance across the countryside, then Inspector Mulligan turned his eyes down and read on.

As you see I am very much alive and intend to stay that way. Harvey I am sorry to tell you is certainly dead and this is what makes me want to pull out though I do not see how. I will find a way. I am sick about Harvey who was as straight as they come and would have had a big future in any Mining Company you like to name. I never guessed there would be anything like this when I got into it, you will know that is true, because you know me, I would have stayed clean. Harvey

*was murdered by a couple of hoods on the orders of
Skipper Ogden—*

'Read that again,' O'Malley said.

Mulligan did so.

'Go on,' said O'Malley.

*The only reason I have come back to Ireland is to
warn Henry Butt to get the hell out or the same will be
done to him. If it had not been for what happened to
Harvey you and I would have a nice 'nest egg' and be
off with the kids in Mexico or Paris or anywhere you
like. With luck we still will. I am not trying to make
excuses because I know I haven't 'played it down the
middle' but what you have to understand is that when
this thing started rolling I did not dream there would
be killing and at no time have I had part of it.*

Mulligan looked up.

'What?' O'Malley said.

'What time d'you imagine he wrote this?'

'Before he killed Gore.'

'You think he did that?'

'Don't you?'

'I do. But I can't fathom why.'

'Read on, perhaps he'll say.'

'Fifty to one he'll not.'

'Is that the end?'

'Not a bit. Wait.'

Mulligan read:

*You will remember when I wrote last I said I thought
I might be on to something pretty hot way up at the
northern end of the site. I could not say more because
if it worked out I could not put anything in writing
and to be honest I was not 100 per cent certain anyway,*

it is some time since I saw cinnabar and when you find what looks like cinnabar in a place like Ireland it sort of throws you, even though when you figure it the conditions are okay, right here on the edge of the Galtee they are anyway. You do not have to tell me I should have reported the cinnabar to Toronto just like I give them the lead and zinc results, that is what my salary is about, but when you find cinnabar like that, and what looks like a damn rich streak, you are 'off balance'. I phoned Moeller-Ansbacher in Zurich which is an Engineering Conglomerate, they do precision stuff and they do a lot in armaments. Fact is I still am not sure whether they are mainly engineering or mainly finance, but I knew about the armaments from the Business Pages. There were other people I could have tried, the truth is I did not suppose it mattered, it all seemed a 'long shot'. I never reckoned anything would come of it and most ways I hoped nothing would. What I figured was if I could find somebody big interested in mercury—that is what you get from cinnabar—and hand them their own personal supply 'on a plate', I would get compensated, it would be like naming my own price. The phoning and cabling do not matter but word must have got to a Mr Big because next day (February 27) I met a Mr Beit in Dublin, then he flew back to Zurich with samples of cinnabar, and next day he was back again, we had lunch at the Russell, and I had a deal. What it came to was I was to get a quarter of a million American dollars (250,000) to keep my mouth shut. To put it 'in a nutshell', they were interested. They aim to buy the site from Ivernia, how they do it is their business but I guess they have to be tempting but not too tempting so Ivernia gets suspicious. Beit did not say much and if you want to know I did not ask, but he mentioned the usefulness of mercury supplies within the Common Market, not having to go to Spain or Mexico or the States, though whether this was just chat I could not say. I figure once these guys can put together their own detonators they are 'home and dry', they are self-contained, you name your order, 50,000 tank shells size 10 or whatever, and they manufacture from scratch. The one snag was I was to quit Ivernia. Not quit like three months' notice, with a quarter million I did not intend hanging around thank you, but quit right away. I was to get a gun and fire it and leave it some place near my room, I was to bust up the drilling rig, then to Zurich to meet the boys and collect. The gun thing seemed crazy, yet all along they seemed to know what they were doing, and Beit said that me missing, the gun, and the demolition job on the rig, was Psychology, sort of salesmanship aimed at getting Ivernia nervous and confused and ready to say, hell, here's a good offer, let's take it and get out. I said nuts—that is to say, I thought it, I did not say it—but went along. You must believe I did not guess the Psychology was to be tougher than just a smashed rig and a gun and me missing. As you know now this was only the start because my successor was to be murdered, they had it all layed 'on the line', and if Harvey had a successor he would be killed too, and so on, just like that, until Ivernia cracked and sold. I have been thinking this could happen only in the Twentieth Century, in the 1970s, but you will say that is cynical, I know you. The idea was this kind of 'Reign of Terror' to scare Ivernia off. I knew nothing about Harvey being killed until the day before yesterday, in Zurich, the guy who let it out does not matter, he is a Swiss Director name of Herder and I think he is trying to frighten me because I am beginning to get 'bugged' by Zurich and these people. The fact Butt is next on the list is why I am here. I told Herder I was going to London for two days to case the investment scene, which is talk they understand. I am scared but once I find Butt to give him the tip I will get back to Zurich. I want my money and out and as I say things may be okay. The moment I have 'cash in hand' I will let you know, and what you can do is check all passports.

'He's quite a letter-writer,' O'Malley murmured.

Mulligan had paused to turn the page. The car had completed a circuit of back roads and was passing for the second time the pillared entrance to the Carrigann Park Hotel's drive. Search-parties of guards were to be seen, and on the roads early arrivals for Mass, but no Henry Butt or Skipper Ogden. The short-wave radio crackled sporadically with negative information.

I have a suite in a hotel called the Gruber with a view over Lake Zurich and am in the 'lap of luxury' so do not worry. For the record, I do not think Moeller-Ansbacher is buying Ivernia, it is a Consortium here named Vogel, Stoffel and Baumann, though Moeller-Ansbacher may be tied in somewhere.

Mulligan paused, looked at O'Malley, and said, 'James Joyce.'

'What about James Joyce?'

'He's buried in Zurich.'

'Is that so?' O'Malley, interested, hoisted the jutting

eyebrows. 'I know he's not in Glasnevin. I hadn't thought where he was.'

'Zurich. He did a lot of his literary work in Zurich. *Ulysses* and all that. Zurich and Paris.'

'John, I think you're right. Are you a Joyceian?'

'I am. You should go to the museum in that Martello Tower at Sandycove. They've got his manuscripts and letters—and his death mask.'

'Is that the truth?'

'I recommend it.'

'I'll go. I will.' O'Malley sat nodding his head, reflecting, wishing himself at Sandycove. 'Read on so. Your man McGrew's as great a windbag as Joyce.'

As far as I can make out Skipper Ogden is the Big Wheel in the Consortium. I guess with him in it is worldwide instead of just Common Market. The first I knew he was part of it—first time I've ever seen him—was when Herder and Beit took me to dinner and there was Ogden, passing through Zurich and wanting to say 'Hi', so he said. He was 'toujours gai' (I wonder is he on drugs?) and though he did not talk much 'business', he had a steak then left, he said me going missing was his instruction because it would help him sway Ivernia shareholders over the Carrigann sell-out. I am sure killing Harvey and now Butt is also all Ogden. The man is a 'Psychopath'. He does not mind my knowing he is behind the deal as I am 'safe', the moment I open my mouth I convict myself, in fact my knowing about him feeds his ego and he likes that, but if he thought I might 'double-cross' it would be 'curtains'. It is no coincidence the armaments group I got in touch with had Ogden on the board because I am not sure Moeller-Ansbacher

*do, but Ogden got wind of it, with his network that
does not surprise me, then he moved in with this Consortium and took the whole deal over. What he is doing
is transferring the Carrigann site from Ivernia to Vogel,
Stoffel and Baumann, selling it to himself, because my
theory is his image. He wants to keep the loot but he is
campaigning as you know on this peace ticket for the
Ohio White House, so he cannot be associated with
mercury which is going to make detonators and bombs.
That may be crazy but so is Ogden. As I see it the only
way he can be stopped is if I talk, which he knows I
must not if I want to stay out of gaol, but it puts me in
a tricky position with Ogden. Once Butt is okay and
I have my 'compensation' and you and I are together
we will burn this letter but until then please tuck it away.
You will—*

Mulligan fell silent.

'Yes, what will she?' O'Malley said.

'That's all,' Mulligan said.

'Is it now. So that's the point Gore arrived.'

'That,' Mulligan agreed, 'might be the moment he
stumbled on his old guest. And of course recognized
him. Quite a moment.'

'For both of them. There must have been a rare old
set-to.'

'There must. McGrew doesn't sound cold-blooded.'
Mulligan folded the letter. 'Still, he'd a fair amount at
stake.'

O'Malley imagined the dawn meeting at the third
green: prying Gore discovering the supposedly dead
McGrew in the act of letter-writing, McGrew desperate
because of discovery. The fair amount at stake had

been McGrew's life. Once it was generally known he
was alive, at large, exhibit number one, he would have
been too dangerous to the Yank, Ogden, to be allowed
to live. Dangerous Dan McGrew, right enough. For the
sake of his own skin, a mortal danger to anyone silly
enough to discover him alive, well and letter-writing by
the third green. So he had plucked up the golf pin.

'We've no proof,' Inspector Mulligan said.

'His prints will be on the pin, see if they're not.'

Mulligan grunted in accord. Superintendent O'Malley gazed through the window at sheep in a field. The
driver had halted at a crossroads and was interrogating
a pair of guards on topography.

O'Malley said, "Tis a well-written letter so. There'll
be changes by evening on the board of Anstruther and
Vogel.'

'Vogel, Stoffel and Baumann.'

'Correct. Which was Anstruther? You had an Anstruther in there.'

'Moeller-Ansbacher was the first contact. They passed
him on.'

'Ah, yes. You've a mind like a steel trap, John. So
what does our man Ogden hope to gain out of all this?'

'A mercury mine.' Patiently, Inspector Mulligan
spelled it out. 'If I understand the letter, Ogden aimed
to sell his Ivernia fields to this Swiss consortium which
he controls. Because if the voters in Ohio thought he
was making bombs with his mercury, and selling them
anywhere, they might vote in someone else. So to prod
the Ivernia board into selling, Ogden stirs up skulldug-
gery in Carrigann and begins disposing of Ivernia geologists. The more dead geologists the merrier until the

board backs out.'

'Exactly so.' O'Malley nodded vigorously. 'Why couldn't McGrew have said just that.'

'It was a longish letter. I don't blame you at all for dozing off.'

'I did not doze off! Not for a tick. I heard every word.' The car moved on. A whitewashed cottage replaced the sheep, and in its turn was gone. 'But I'll tell you, I did have a bit of a vision.'

'I see.'

'You don't either. 'Twas not a dream.'

'No, no. A vision.'

'Ara, you'll not understand. Like a picture, like one of those lantern-slides when we were lads. There were these dogs.'

'Dogs.'

'Ay, dogs, what's wrong with dogs? I can't help it, can I? 'Tis not my fault if I have a vision of dogs.'

CHAPTER XXII

There was a key, which was convenient. (Other conveniences, such as brakes, were lacking, but Farmer Butt, examining the vehicle in haste, was not to discover this until later.) Headlights, painted registration number, steering-wheel, a handle behind the steering-wheel which might be lights, hooter, anything really (it was, in fact, for attaching wagons, harrows and sprinklers), clutch pedal, and gear, or to be exact, two gears. (To be absolutely exact—and to be absolutely exact

Henry, scrutinizing, rubbed earth from the two letters H embossed on the iron plate beside the two gears— there were two gear levers and eight gears. He would, he imagined, need them all.) The front wheels were small, the rear wheels ludicrously big. On the springy perforated seat, cast in iron for a Goliath's buttocks, lay a folded sack, a touch of luxury judged by Henry to be inspired. Not for one moment did he expect this derelict engine to go. If it went, why was the field stubble? Why had the tractor not ploughed the field, the good seed not been scattered on the land? Henry switched on the ignition. The tractor vibrated with rowdy joy.

He climbed aboard. The amiable rumbling of a tractor, like mooing cows, or a tipped cider bottle clinking against the labourer's teeth, was one of several unremarked sounds integral to the pastoral scene, Henry had always thought. A tractor between the knees, he discovered, was something else. The engine bellowed, unsecured parts clattered, the ground trembled. Henry pulsated in goliath's seat. Not only Skipper Ogden but all County Cork together with adjacent counties to north, east and west could not have helped but sit up and wonder.

If Ogden shoots, I won't hear a thing, thought Henry, giving the shaking steering-wheel an experimental twist. He dug in his pocket for snuff.

Snuff at this pressing moment was only minimally a gesture, a last embattled symbol of civilized man flung in the face, so to speak, of the barbarian with the gun. Henry's head, woozy with fatigue and apprehension, really did need clearing. If I am to journey once more, he vowed, I shall journey with a clear head.

'Aaaaaaaaaaaaghsssssh!' inaudibly trumpeted Henry, the sneeze gulped and swallowed in the tractor's roar.

He depressed the clutch, wrenched a gear lever, released the clutch. The tractor lurched backwards and continued backwards through the stubble.

Rather than mess with gears at a time when all endeavour had to be concentrated on keeping his seat, Henry allowed the machine to travel. The tractor shuddered as it regressed, whether from the uneven ground or because this was the way of tractors, its rider did not know. Glancing over his shoulder, Henry saw acres of space. He faced forward again, towards the receding spinney, imploring himself to relax, be cool. Head up, elbows in, back straight but not rigid, steering-wheel held firmly but not tautly, Henry trundled backwards through the stubble. His cheeks wobbled, his body bounced. The wheel was set flat like a bus driver's, and vaguely he wondered whether bus driving was more or less of a knack than tractor driving. He looked at the travelling ground beneath him and estimated that he was slightly closer to it than when he had been atop Dobbin. Were horses or tractors the more threatening to the rider? All Henry knew of tractors was their propensity for turning over and grinding the driver into the ground.

Ogden in doeskin jacket, a distant figure with cradled shotgun, emerged from the Carrigann end of the spinney. Ogden and Henry gazed at each other across the bristly field. The sun had climbed another ten degrees.

He'll have a job hitting me at this range, he'll only bring the cops, Henry thought, hopefully and correctly, and half-hoping that Ogden might shoot and bring the cops.

Instead of shooting, Ogden ran along the edge of the spinney. Henry watched him disappear through a hedge extending at right-angles from the spinney and forming a border along one side of the stubble-field. He can't be running away, Henry reasoned, again correctly; but if he runs the whole length of the hedge, then back into the field, and I keep on course, we shall bump into each other.

No more with Ogden than McGrew, Henry decided, would there be a chance for rational discussion, for arguing that bullets might as well be spared because the mercury discovery was blown. Apart from the fatuity of discussing anything with a nut, nothing could be discussed in competition with the racket from the tractor's engine. If he stopped the engine he would be a stranded turkey, the next trophy on the roll-call of dead geologists. Cautiously, Henry turned the steering-wheel.

The tractor responded, bending through forty-five degrees and trundling backwards along a line diagonally away from the hedge. Behind the hedge, a sparkle of sun on metal caught Henry's eye. But more urgent were the obstacles he was approaching: the field's corner, a shallow ditch, and a stack of sacks of loam or lime. The tractor shaved the sacks, jolted into and out of the ditch, and reverberated into the next field, which had been ploughed.

Henry's glasses had become tinted with sweat and flung mud. He wiped them with a thumb. The time had come, he conceded, to go forwards.

As the pedal which he pressed with his left foot, and which he believed might be a brake, accomplished nothing, he switched off the ignition. Had the owner for-

saken his machine while acquiring a new brake? The
tractor bumped at decreasing speed over furrows, then
halted lop-sidedly, like a beached yacht. Silence lapped
over Henry like water. Faintly, somewhere, tolled a
church bell. He turned the key, resuscitating the engine.
He pushed the gear lever into a random slot. The
tractor moved forwards. Turning the wheel, Henry
headed away from Ogden's hedge and onwards, mightily
vibrating, to fresh woods and pastures new.

Beyond the next field stood telegraph poles and so,
presumably, a road. Henry reckoned the road must be
the Carrigann road, or at any rate a road which would
lead to Carrigann, if he pointed the right way. Elbows
well in, spine beginning to curve, Henry glanced about
him for landmarks and saw none. Looking back, he
could not see the spinney. Ogden, with gun, was half
an acre away, sprinting in the tractor's wake.

Henry mashed his shoe on the clutch and sought a
higher gear, but the new slot made no appreciable
difference to the tractor's speed, and removal of a hand
from the wheel caused him to sway abominably. He
felt a jolt and heard above the engine's din a clang.
Looking back once more, he saw Ogden with the gun
at his shoulder, shooting.

Henry's spine curved like a coathanger over the
steering-wheel. Bent low, he kept going, there being
nothing else to do. The tractor persevered. Ahead, above
the broken brim of the hedge from which rose telegraph
poles, moved a white roof, the Cadillac, driver Kinsella
absolute in his quest for priests. The tractor, having left
the ploughed field by way of an established tractor track,
now advanced through pasture. The gate where cows

had assembled at the field's far end was visibly shut, and sooner than risk an encounter with padlocked iron, Henry headed for the hedge, searching for a gap.

He found a one-yard gap and aimed his juggernaut towards it. The tractor tore through the hedge and down a verdant bank. Such was the impetus given by this bank that the tractor hurtled across the road and half-way up the opposite bank, where it stalled, then began to roll backwards. Henry clung to the wheel, certain he ought to jump but not daring to. The tractor came to rest crosswise on the hump of the road.

Quaking, closing his mind to alternatives and prospects, trusting now to instinct, Henry switched on the ignition, fiddled the wheel and gears—this time the second, untried gear lever—and set off along the empty road. He risked a hand off the wheel to experiment with the gear. The hedges whisked by. Whatever gear he had found was high, if not top. After a succession of belching, bounding movements, the tractor gathered itself, sprang, then rumbled berserk along the middle of the road. Vainly Henry pumped what had to be, surely, the foot-brake. He pulled and pushed at the lever behind the steering-wheel, achieving not a diminution in speed but, at the rear of the tractor, a rasping effect which would have detached a ploughshare, had there been one. In two attempts to shift the gear lever he succeeded only in eliciting a monstrous grinding like the jaws of Cerberus. He brought both hands to the steering-wheel as a bend in the road volleyed towards him. Round the bend, two guards crowded back into the hedge.

Dumbly, Henry screamed at the guards that he was

having trouble, that somewhere was Ogden, that the brakes were faulty. A blaring Armageddon of tractor-roar engulfed his words. As he swept by, one of the guards saluted.

There came a second twist in the road, then a third. At thirty miles an hour, which seemed from the tractor's seat one hundred and thirty, Henry drove past cottages. Suddenly there were parked cars at the roadside. Then more parked cars, walking people, a bounding cat, pavements and painted buildings, a car in the road's centre, hazards of every kind. And now people who did not walk but scuttled sensibly, out of his path. By the time he had oriented himself to the fact that he was entering Carrigann not from the north, past the Carrigann Park Hotel, as he had expected, but from the south, he was half-way along the main street. The car in the middle of the road reversed on to the pavement as though stung. The way ahead was cleared for him: Caesar returning in triumph through Rome.

Henry was blearily aware that the blur of people wore smart coats and hats, navy-blue suits with white shirts, and that they were going to or coming from Mass. That explained the numbers. He concentrated on steering straight and not killing anyone. Elbows in, back straight, Henry thundered through Carrigann. He uttered a token shout apropos brakes but the token was whipped up and away, over the rooftops like paper in a wind. He wondered whether the spectators were shouting back words of encouragement. Or perhaps threatening slogans like 'Go home, Butt!' Egan's rushed past. Then Henry spotted Kate.

She stood on the pavement, staring, isolated among

blue uniforms and a plainclothes cop whom Henry thought he recognized. O'Hara possibly? She was in red. Was she off to Mass? Henry wore a nervous smile of greeting and lifted a hand from the steering-wheel, though by the time the hand was up he had vibrated past. For a moment the arm stayed aloft in salutation, then dropped to the steering-wheel and wrenched.

He took the corner like a rally driver. In front the road was less thickly populated, but he had to wrench again to skirt an old shawled woman carrying a missal. She hopped aside in a flurry of shawl and spilled bookmarks. A car was approaching, a rattling, charred saloon with yellow mudguards and painted inscriptions, and Henry hunted in desperation for the horn.

By now he accepted that his tractor would stop, eventually, in one of two ways: by running out of petrol, or colliding with something, such as the approaching taxi. He could turn off the ignition, but that was no answer to the present crisis. He steered to the right, oblivious of the Irish rule of the road. Billy Dunne's saloon, no longer knowing which way to steer, made an emergency stop in the dead centre of the road and closed, figuratively, its eyes. The tractor sheered past, collecting a doorhandle. Henry glimpsed in the vehicle's interior a startled face under a peaked cap, and in the rear seat, looking out at the tractor and its rider, Ogden.

Game as its rider, the tractor soldiered on. None the less, life's swindle, the fraud of it all, a concept hitherto foreign to Henry's buoyant disposition, came home to him.

Here he was on a tractor he could not control. There was Ogden, mass murderer of geologists, travelling by cab. Glancing round, Henry saw the taxi performing a U-turn. Farther back along the road, wailing into view round a corner of Carrigann's crossroads, came a garda car. Henry looked front and twisted the steering-wheel hard to the right.

The tractor roared between stone pillars, one of them bearing the tidings, CARRIGANN PARK HOTEL. SELECT ACCOMMODATION. Ahead, impeccably proportioned at the end of the drive, stood a sort of haven, unless flood, dry-rot or the hand of God demolished it during the next sixty seconds, which to Henry in his new bleak mood seemed likely. Behind him the closing taxi, Ogden aboard, started to sound its horn. More distantly the garda car's siren howled like a wolf.

The bunkered, moon-cratered surface of the drive foiled three attempts to switch off the ignition. Each time Henry's hand reached for the key the tractor bounced into another foxhole, and to keep his balance the hand flew back to the steering-wheel. By the time he had turned the key the front steps of Carrigann Park loomed above him. Co-proprietor Flynn, trudging down the steps with a mattress on his back, watched with interest, trying to remember if agricultural work was due to begin, and who might have summoned Billy Dunne, and what the guards were after. Henry twisted the steering-wheel. With only fractionally diminishing speed the tractor followed the drive along the front of the hotel, then round the side. Here, abruptly, against a sombre green wall of vegetable matter, the drive ended.

The tractor ploughed through rhododendron bushes and emerged, slowing, in a lesser undergrowth of brambles and nettles. On a cinder path beside an arched gateway in a stone wall, it expired. Now that the tractor was at peace, the church bell and the garda car's siren alone filled the air. There was no sound of Billy Dunne's taxi.

Henry climbed down. On the ground he discovered to his surprise that he was not on his feet but on his knees. Looking back at the flattened swathe left by the tractor he saw, fifty yards away over the tops of the rhododendrons, the gun, and Ogden's face regarding him. He wondered whether Ogden were near enough to take a shot.

Henry lumbered to his feet, wobbled, then lurched towards, and past, the arch in the wall.

He managed to change direction and career through the arch at the moment the safari gun fired and some manner of African rhinoceros pellet struck him.

CHAPTER XXIII

General Grant, Hayes, Garfield (assassinated), McKinley (assassinated), Taft, Harding.

Six. Had he missed anyone? Was Harrison from Ohio? Grant had been elected from Illinois but he was Ohio-born, Point Pleasant, so he counted, in a way.

The fevered musings of Henry Butt, face down in the Mato Grosso of the walled garden, shifted from French cuisine to American Presidents from Ohio, and back to French cuisine. *Gratin de cervelles. Coquilles St Jacques à la Parisienne,* with a cool Chablis, or better still a Montrachet, which had been the favourite wine of John Foster Dulles, he had read somewhere, long, long ago.

Henry listened to the siren's persistent, fatuous wail, church bells, confused shouting, the trampling of Ogden. The pain was becoming localized down the left side, perhaps even in the arm alone. He still wore his glasses. They were like an additional limb, Henry thought. Separable from him only by death or magic.

The injustice did not plague him any more. Henry knew, a little spitefully, that Skipper Ogden would never now become the seventh Buckeye President. Ogden would be lucky if he kept out of gaol. Would it be an Irish gaol or an American gaol? Probably it would be a hospital with bars. To shoot first and explain later, to need so keenly and obsessively to keep the cinnabar secret, which had he but known was no longer a secret, the man had to be mad as a hatter.

The trampling was close, imminent. Henry rose to his knees, then to his feet. Someone should have told Ogden that the Sudbury Butts were battlers to the end. If the end were to be now, there would have to be the price of more rhinoceros pellets. Henry staggered through the jungle.

Grant had been a traveller too, before he went bankrupt. One bankrupt, two assassinated, and of genial Warren Gamaliel Harding the less said the better. They hadn't exactly shone, the Ohio boys. If Ogden could become the third Ohio President to be assassinated, maybe he would be worth electing.

Henry leaned breathless against a tree, unsure whether the rustling was his own breathing, or Ogden.

Boeuf à la mode en gelée, that was the meal, with a

light claret, room temperature, like a Pomerol, nothing nicer. Had he eaten anything at all since arriving in Ireland? Yes, he had. Steak and tea at Evangeline's in Mallow, with darling Kate, and poor Garda Griffin. Biscuits somewhere. A sandwich.

Henry weaved towards the shed which leaned against the walled garden's farthest wall. There were dogs inside, he could hear them, and he wondered if he could not perhaps smell them too. But he did not mind dogs. He would shelter with dogs from Ogden. If Ogden wanted to come into the shed after him, Ogden would have to shift a door held shut by two hundred and fifteen pounds of avoirdupois. Plus dogs.

Distantly, above the yowling of Cooney's starved greyhounds, rose the siren's wail.

Virginia had the record number of Presidents, beating Ohio by one or two, he could have listed them once. Henry fumbled with the catch on the shed door. North American history had been his hobby, many years ago. Given time and a glass of wine he might still have listed the Virginia Presidents, their dates, parties, the names of their wives.

The door swung open and Henry swung backwards with it, reeling in an arc against the side of the shed as the hounds of hell burst from night into day. Henry dropped, comfortably squeezed between the open door and the side of the shed. The greyhounds flowed out, yelping and howling, following their leader and Henry's trail of blood towards Ogden, who stalked with gun through briars and tattered apple trees.

Virginia had George Washington, Jefferson, Madison, Monroe . . .

The disgusting part, Henry discovered, was the stink. From the open door, in the wake of the dogs, poured in a torrent the most sickening, putrescent perfume he had ever known. One of the last dogs, one of the condemned four on the co-proprietors' auction list, had found him, lying on his side between the door and the side of the shed, and was licking his cheeks. After a moment the dog raced after its pals.

The pals might have licked Ogden too, but Ogden fired his sixteen-bore safari gun into them, blasting a wide hole in the head of the leader, peppering the runners-up, and causing the more timorous to scatter. Others sprang at him, yowling and snarling. Ogden fell, the scattered greyhounds returned, and the entire pack swarmed over him before arriving guards, co-proprietors and oddments of guests could do much about it.

Wondering, not deeply, whether it was a stretcher, or the mattress Flynn had humped, on to which he was being lifted, Henry shut his eyes and let others take over. The siren and the tolling bell were silent, but there were many voices, and far away the yapping of dogs. He was curious to know, though again not deeply, whether the dogs merely sounded far away, because he was dying and his senses were leaving him, or were they in fact fields away, in flight, pursued by Cooney across the rolling grasslands of County Cork?

In the hotel a dispute arose over where he should be put now. They chose the camp-bed in a heaped junk-room which was Kate's room. Kate, when he spotted her, was having trouble with a music-stand; she was trying to move it aside but one of its prongs was trapped under the vent of Flynn's jacket, and as Flynn, unaware, was buttoning his jacket, Kate could free the prong only at the risk of stabbing him in the back. She wore an immaculate foot-bandage, a burgundy-red Sunday dress, and her black hair was pinned again, brushed straight back and tied with something behind.

'That's a great outfit,' Henry told her. 'Cheerful.'

'Still a moment, Henry, please,' weary Dr Langer said, dabbing antiseptic.

Henry kept his eyes on Kate but heard, above him, on the other side of the camp-bed, O'Malley.

'I told you,' O'Malley was saying. 'Didn't I tell you I dreamed the dogs?'

'A vision, you said,' said Mulligan.

'That's what I said,' said O'Malley.

'What,' Henry interrupted, 'happened to Ogden?'

''Tis too early to say. He might live.' Superintendent O'Malley wore an anxious air. He had not removed his hat. 'Lie easy now, Mr Butt. Don't be talking. Do as the doctor says.'

'I thought there was something funny.' Billy Dunne in peaked cap justified himself with energy to the assembly at large. 'He had this gun, see, but I thought he'd be after the rabbits. You meet all sorts in the taxicab trade.'

Henry, eyes level with topaz knees, asked the doctor, 'How am I?'

Above the topaz bulged an Aran-jerseyed paunch. Dr Langer bandaged with hands calloused by niblick and mashie swinging; interrupted and ruined swinging (he would never vacation in Ireland again), but swinging none the less. It wasn't, he explained, too bad. The main trouble had been a stone splinter, a big one, where the shot had hit the archway, though he knew nothing about shot himself. There'd have to be an X-ray. It was the elbow. Some nicks in other places, but mainly the elbow.

'The trochlea,' Kate said smugly.

'Trochlea,' echoed Henry. 'Is that so?'

Kate nodded.

'Listen,' said Henry, 'have you spoken to Father Fahy yet?'

'You're a terrible eager man,' said Kate. 'We'll speak to him together.'